*Redless rooms and shallow halls*
*Are what I now call home*
*'Neath verdant skies and azure fields*
*E'er shall I roam.*

# WORLD WITHOUT RED

Volume 1:
*The Taking of Red*

## J. P. Cloud

iUniverse, Inc.
Bloomington

World Without Red
Volume 1: The Taking of Red
FIRST EDITION

iUniverse books may be ordered through booksellers or by contacting:

iUniverse
1663 Liberty Drive
Bloomington, IN 47403
www.iuniverse.com
1-800-Authors (1-800-288-4677)

ISBN: 978-1-4502-6696-3 (sc)
ISBN: 978-1-4502-6702-1 (e)

Printed in the United States of America

iUniverse rev. date: 8/19/2011

*To my mother, Red Cloud*

## NOTE

The main action of the story takes place in the near future.

# INTRODUCTION

---

This is a story about gratitude.

We all believe that we are grateful for the basic necessities of life. The food, the money, a roof over our heads, the sun shining in the blue sky, the air we breathe, sound and vision. These are the "little things" that we like to believe we are thankful and grateful for.

But are we, *really?*

What if we all lost something we take for granted every day in our lives?

What if we all suddenly lost something that had always been there for us, for eons? We've all had *take-aways* happen to us; a certain job or situation where, in the beginning, the perks and goodies that made the job so attractive were gradually taken away one-by-one by management. The take-aways always happened, sooner or later. But what if one day, a *really, big* take-away happened? What if God, Nature and the Universe at the Great Office Meeting in the Sky, decided to make one *huge* take-away, for not reason at all?

What if they took away *beauty?* What if everyone and everything on Earth looked flat, dull and lifeless? What if everyone on Earth appeared equally *ugly?*

A "red" apple is red *only in our minds.* The brain perceives color through wavelengths and frequencies. What if one of those wavelengths that we take for granted every day was shattered?

This is the story of Martin Boes. Martin Boes- genius inventor, scientist, astronomer, billionaire and humanitarian, all rolled into one man! There were some that called him *Wizard*. This is the story of the comet with his name on it, and what the comet did, and how Martin Boes, with all his genius inventiveness, scientific knowledge and vast wealth was only human, and powerless to prevent what happened.

*Loss!* It's such a cold, hard word, cold and hard as steel! The *loss* of a loved one. The *loss* of money. The *loss* of time. We have all suffered some great loss at some point in our lives. This is a story about a great loss, and how people would adapt to the loss- *or not*.

—J.P. Cloud
July, 2011

# CONTENTS

# CHAPTER 1

## Red Family

JOSH PICKED UP his red plastic toothbrush and squeezed out some red-striped toothpaste onto it. He wet it a little, and looking into the bathroom mirror, started brushing in the sawing motion that he was always told not to do, remembered, and started brushing in the up-and-down motion that he was always told to do. After a few seconds, he switched back to the back and forth motion that he was always told not to do.

Josh was in the Immaculate Bathroom, the upstairs bathroom everyone liked to use in the morning. Mom kept it spotless, pristine. There was always blue water in the Immaculate Bathroom toilet. He rinsed and smiled in the mirror. *"Lookin' good!"* he thought his Dad would say. He opened the mirror door and grabbed the Brylcreem tube. He squeezed out a little dab of it onto his hand and rubbed it into his palms. He ran his hands through his thick, wavy red hair, which was his family's trait, except for Dad, who had brown hair. His Dad gave him the Brylcreem. *"A little dab'll do ya!"* his Dad told Josh, repeating the memorable tagline. It was true. More than a little dab made your hair greasy, which attracted dirt. Josh liked the smell of it. He combed his hair and washed his hands just in time for Jodie to knock on the door.

"My turn", said his sister, who was also waiting to get ready for school. "I'm outta here", said Josh, closing the cabinet and pushing past Jodie, like he always did. Jodie replaced Josh in the mirror and got ready. She switched on the red plastic radio and her favorite song was on. "All right!" she yelled, opening the mirror door and grabbing her make-up. She was fifteen. She didn't need much make-up. She was beautiful, but she didn't think so. She wouldn't go anywhere without make-up. She didn't like her freckles, but they were few and easily covered. She had no teen acne problem, so no zit cream for her. Next, she used eye-liner and mascara, though she really didn't need it. But it did make a difference. Next, came her hair. Jodie had thick, lush long red hair that hung down her back to her waist. It was gorgeous. If she were just a little older, she could have easily been of those "hair models" seen on TV hair product commercials. All the boys at school loved her long red hair. She did realize that she was becoming more and more popular with the boys.

She combed and brushed her hair, being careful for tangles. Most of the time, she would put her hair up in a bun or in braids, but today she liked herself, so she let it down. She sneaked a dab of Brylcreem, too, and rubbed it in her palms and applied it to her temples so her hair wouldn't flop in her face, but created a sexy forelock that dipped just above the eyelid, like she had seen in her teen magazines. She shook her hair. She was perfect. Her ever- burgeoning bosom was all-the-more apparent in her red sweater. Another of her favorite songs came on. "Yes!" she breathed, and added some pale red lip gloss. She smacked her lips, washed her hands and was off, motivated to school with her favorite song, good to go. Her timing was just right; her Mom knocked on the door. "My turn now" said her mother, cheerily. When Jodie opened the bathroom door, her mother was taken aback. *Who was this young woman in our bathroom?* Jodie started to leave, but her mother stopped her. "What?' asked Jodie? Her mother just looked at her with a dreamy look. "Too much cleavage?"

"Oh! No, no, you look fine", her mother said at last. I can't believe how much you've grown! I can't believe how much you... how much you look like me... you were just a little girl a couple months ago, at least it seems... don't forget your scarf and gloves, it's going to be cold today."

"You always *say* that", sighed Jodie.

"I always say it, because you always forget", replied her mother.

"Whatever."

"You have a nice day, honey." She hugged and kissed her daughter warmly. "You too, Mom. Love you. Bye."

"Love you, too. Bye-bye."She watched her daughter leave, still amazed at how she looked like a young woman. It all just somehow escaped her notice. She knew Jodie was experimenting with sex. Jodie did look very much like her mother, for her mother was still a beauty, a wife and mother to die for. Her thick red hair was just as lustrous as her daughter's, though not as long. She watched what she ate and worked out to keep her "girlish physique", as she would joke. She had never smoked, or drank too much. She worked at and managed her two story house with the red shingled roof, while her husband was at work at *Inland Northwest Shed and Storage.* She kept a magnificent kitchen and was a great cook. She played guitar and sang, mostly country songs. She also fancied herself as a writer, and she was quite good. She often sold freelance articles to local newspapers and magazines. She and Jimbo both loved country songs and encouraged the kids to listen. She felt country music was positive, family friendly, and darn good music! Her immaculate bathrooms were the talk of the neighborhood with its antique maps and French Barrister prints. She kept blue water in *all* her toilets. She enjoyed having coffee looking out her front window at her garden arrangements, listening to all the latest books on CD. From her front window, she could see the entire neighborhood. She could watch the Northwest birds frolicking, like the Quail, red-headed woodpeckers and the brick-red breasted Robins.

One day, she noticed some new neighbors moving in across the street. She watched as movers unloaded the furniture, wondered if she should go over and welcome them to the neighborhood. Her new neighbors were an older lady and a middle-aged man. The man was very short in height, about five feet, two inches. He had long gray hair but was bald on top, and had a long gray beard. With his red backward baseball cap, he looked like one of Santa's Elves. He was very energetic and hard-working. Over the next few days, and then weeks, she would always see the Elfin Man hard at work doing something. He'd be out there either mowing his lawn, edging it, weed-eating it, working on the garden, sawing wood, or making cabinets and frames. He seemed to never stop. He was even more anal about his garden and lawn than Bren was. She smiled to herself. She was glad and relieved that her new neighbors worked hard and cared about their homes and properties. But she wondered that they put so much work into the yard, yet never enjoyed it. Although they had expensive whicker lounge chairs with plump cushions on their front porch, the Elfin Man and his mother were never seen out on their porch or patio. Then one day, she saw the Elfin Man pull up in his driveway in a classic Candy Apple Red 1964 Corvette Stingray! Her husband Jim would *die* when he saw it! He had a life-long dream to get a Stinger like that. Jim was an expert on Chevys and especially Corvettes. He loved them. *"Okay, now we'll have something to talk about with the neighbors"* The elfin man opened the automatic garage door and drove in the Red Stingray. She couldn't wait for Jimbo to get home.

# CHAPTER 2

## Something Was Not Right

**M**ARTIN BOES BLINKED. Something was not right. He re-adjusted his telescopic eye-piece and looked again. He squinted at the dim celestial body still far out in space. The celestial body was in a place where it was not supposed to be in its projected orbit through the solar system. But there it was, for Martin Boes and the entire world to see. *A comet.*

He had seen comets before, had tracked them since he was a student. But this comet was a different sort of comet, a comet that was special and personal to Martin Boes. After all, it had *his* name on it. Martin Boes compared the comet's previous location to the current one on its long, long elliptical orbit. It was somehow off course. He looked hard and long, deep into the telescope, deep into space. Something *still* wasn't right. He looked again and again in the whole range of magnifications. He was becoming concerned now. He went to the computer and played the script showing the comet's previous projected orbit and trajectory. Then, he created a new script, starring the comet with its new current projected orbit and trajectory. Martin Boes blinked again at the script. It was not good.

The script called for the comet to smash into Earth. Martin

Boes was alarmed. It would have been better had he not known what he knew about comets and asteroids. Knowing what he knew, he knew he was also correct in his figures. Still, he replayed the scripts over and over. The results indicated what he dreaded. The comet was on a collision course with the planet Earth! Something had knocked it off course, maybe a gravitational tug from Jupiter or Saturn. At its current trajectory, the comet would reach Earth in approximately one year. The comet was big, nine miles wide- a planet killer, if it should hit. Martin Boes' heart pounded. He stopped and made some coffee, sat down. Twenty minutes later, he again replayed the scripts and peered through the telescope into deep space. He created a new script again, but it ended up with the same finale. *Ka-boom!*

There was no mistake about it. Although Martin Boes' observatory in his Arizona mountain-top office at was small, it boasted a state-of-the-art telescope that was as good as, or better than any major observatory. It was just as good as the ones that NASA had, or JPL, or CBAT (Central Bureau for Astronomical Telegrams), the International comet tracking agency. He stopped again, poured another cup of coffee. He looked out at the panorama view of Tucson through the window panes made out of ice that wouldn't melt, one of his inventions. He saw a lot from his vantage point. He was amazed at how most people never drew their curtains or shades for privacy. "*They should close their curtains if they don't want people to see them*" he felt. Then he remembered the comet. He hoped, wished and prayed that he was wrong about the projections. He looked at the night skyline and thought about the history of the comet with his name on it.

Though the comet had Martin Boes' name on it, it was not named after him. It was named after its two discoverers, his father Telemon Ajax Boes and his associate, Professor Stilmaker. Martin Boes had been keeping track of the *Boes-Stilmaker Comet* since his father passed away about ten years ago. The comet's orbit was always far away from Earth and it came closest to Earth every sixty-three years. Even then, it could only be seen with the most powerful telescopes. But now, in about a year, the Earth was going to get a *really* good look at the *Boes-Stilmaker Comet!*

Martin Boes gulped down the rest of his lukewarm coffee and thought about what to do. He thought about notifying CBAT, but hesitated, because he might be wrong. Dad was gone now, but he thought about what Dad would do. Dad would probably contact Professor Stilmaker, who had shared the discovery of the Boes-Stilmaker Comet with him nearly forty years ago. Martin Boes picked up his iPhone 7 and punched up the beautiful Soleil, in Los Angeles. She was his sometimes girlfriend. "Hey, you!" cried Soleil, her face popping up on the large, vertical iPhone screen in High Definition 3-D. Her beauty was startling, even to Martin Boes, who had known her for two years, now. He had hired Soleil to run the *Boes-Soleil School of Design*, which was adjacent to Martin Boes Aerodynamics in Los Angeles. HD merely emphasized her beauty. "Hey!" said Martin Boes fascinated how the screen framed her face, capturing the essence of her beauty and personality. She could see him on her iPhone, too. "Watcha doin', big boy?"

"Ohhh, I was just staring out into space, and I thought of you…"

"How cool! Did you see my boobs?"

"*What?* No! Oh, ha ha ha!" he laughed, his face turning red. "Well, too bad, you're really missing out." She loved to tease him. "I know… I mean, I was just looking through the telescope."

"Your face is red… a shy little boy. Were you a shy little boy growing up?"

"No." He was. "I'm not shy with *you*, am I?"

"Nope. Well, sort of.

"So, what's up, Skippy?"

"Oh! I need to contact Professor Stilmaker about something." He wasn't going to tell Soleil about the comet. "Can you please check the files and find out where he is? I haven't seen him since my father's funeral ten years ago. He might still be hanging around JPL, or living in Southern California somewhere."

"Sure, no problem, Boss!" He hated it when people called him *Boss*, and she knew it. "I'll be happy to check, especially if it means you might swing by." She gave him that look, that loving look she gave that made every man she met fall in love with her. Martin Boes was no exception. "I might… I might just do that. I think I'm going to have to, if he's out there."

"I hope he is. I miss you, you handsome devil."

"I bet you say that to all your boyfriends."

"Me? I don't have a boyfriend. My boyfriend is my job. And that's *your* fault."

"What about the rich Sheik guy? What'd you call him? The Emu?"

"The Emir, wise guy! The Emir of Qattara! I'm not joking. You think it's easy for me to find a boyfriend, don't you? Well, it's not."

"Oh stop, you're breaking my heart!" he laughed.

"My iPhone is my boyfriend." She pushed a button and a voice that sounded a lot like Martin Boes said "Would you like to save this video call, Soleil? Press or say save to save. "Save." said Soleil "See? I push its buttons and it does everything I want."

"Everything?"

"All right, smart-ass, just about everything."

"Wish *I* were an iPhone! That iPhone is getting a lot more action than *I* am."

"Well, you're *not!* I push *you*r buttons and you don't do anything I want *at all!*"

"You push my buttons, that's for *damn* sure. Sometimes,

you let me push *your* buttons" He meant her boobs. "What?—Oh, very funny!"

"See, even I can come up with a little humor."

"Very little. OK, Skippy, I'll locate Professor Stilmaker and get right back to you. I'm looking forward to seeing you."

"Me too, H-…" He almost called her *Honey*, and he knew how she hated that. "You almost said *Honey*, didn't you? You know how I hate that. You think I'm kidding?"

"I know. Sorry. Bad habit from the old days. OK, I'll be seeing you soon! Bye, now!"

"Bye! Call you back in a bit!" She winked enticingly and hung up, her face frozen on the last frame of the video. Martin Boes stared at the gorgeous face he was just talking to. He still couldn't believe his luck in finding Soleil. "Would you like to save the last video call?" asked the iPhone, in Soleil's voice. "To save, press or say yes."

"Yes"

"What would you like to save the call as?" asked iPhone/Soleil. "Um… Soleil 36"

"Saving as Um Soleil 36. If this is correct, press or say save."

"Save."

"Um Soleil 36 has been saved. Do you need anything else?"

"Just your naked body in my bed."

"I'm sorry .I did not understand that response. Goodbye." said iPhone/Soleil.

"Good bye, *honey*", said Martin Boes, wistfully.

# CHAPTER 3

## Nightmare in Red

WHEN MARTIN BOES woke up, he was in bed in a strange dark room lit by candles and a roaring fireplace. The flame gave the room a red appearance. The room had red painted shelves and trimming. On the shelves was a selection of Hummels, arranged in a red color scheme. It was very cold. He was on his back, his arms flat by his side. He looked at his bed and he was tucked in very tightly- in fact too tightly, as if he had been restrained. His bed was deep in a coffin-like wooden frame, though not coffin shaped. His blankets and sheets were holding him down. He thought he had been kidnapped again. Still, he was very calm. The fire produced dazzling shadows all round the room. He heard voices coming near; it sounded like children's voices... children's voices singing.

Suddenly, eight children came into the room, singing. They all surrounded Martin Boes in his bed in a Ring-Around-The Rosie formation and danced. They were dressed in red *lederhosen* and traditional European folk costumes. There were red sleigh-bells attached to the costumes. They were beautiful. They were fair haired and rosy cheeked boys and girls, and they sang beautifully. They circled round his bed one way, turned around and circled back the other way. The boys and girls would turn to each other and give little side-kissing motions to each other's faces and pat hands, then dance again.

After eight choruses, the children now in unison produced antique match-safes. Still dancing and singing, they all at once each lit a match on the punched tin part of their match-safes. Their singing, red-cheeked faces waved back and forth as they gazed with delight at their lit matches. They now skipped happily around Martin Boes in his bed, and one-by-one, tossed a lit match onto the bed. Martin Boes watched as the lit matches hit the woolen blanket that was holding him down. He was a little concerned, but not overly so. The children pulled out their match-safes in unison, struck another match. Again, with the delighted, singing faces, they circled around again with a *pas-de-deux*, and threw their lit matches all at once on to the bed. The blankets were starting to catch fire. Martin Boes now wondered what was going on. The children kept circling the flaming bed, still singing and laughing, but at a faster tempo. Martin Boes became alarmed. *"I'm catching on fire!"*

Martin Boes screamed. He struggled to get free, but couldn't move. His bed sheets and blankets held him down, immobile. The red flames became a Viking's funeral pyre as Martin Boes began to burn up. The children ignored him and kept dancing and singing.

Martin Boes woke up for real, gasping. He saw it was a dream, was grateful he wasn't kidnapped again. He wondered why there was so much of the color Red in his dream. He picked up his iPhone 7 to call Soleil and tell her about his Hellish nightmare in Red.

Martin Boes flew to Los Angeles to meet Stilmaker and discuss the wayward comet. He had mentioned the comet to Stilmaker without going into detail, and He said he would look into it. Stilmaker was semi-retired and living in Pasadena, not far from Cal Tech. He told Martin Boes to meet him at the Bonaventure Hotel. Martin Boes met his chauffer and bodyguard Mikey at the airport. Mikey was a big, strong black man who previously was a bouncer in a Hollywood night club. He had been with Martin Boes Aerodynamics for ten years. He was his right-hand man, and was also on the Martin Boes Foundation for Humanity Tribunal board. He was very stolid and serious. He rarely smiled, and it was a miracle to get him to joke and laugh. He was all business, and he was the best at his job of watching over Martin Boes. "Welcome back, sir. How are you today?"

"Fine, Mike, thank you. And yourself?"

"Never better. So nice to see you again, sir. How was it in Arizona? Thought you were going to stay longer. Is everything all right?"

"Fine, except that the comet with my name on it is going to *smash into Earth and kill us all!*" He didn't really say that. That was what he would have said if he were being completely honest. Instead, he said "Fine. I have to see Professor Stilmaker about some earthly matters, so to speak." Mikey drove Martin Boes to the hotel. On the way, he wondered what Stilmaker would say about the wayward comet. It had his name on it, too. Mikey dropped him off at the hotel. As he rode the outside elevator to the 12th floor, he wondered what Stilmaker would say. Would he agree with him to alert the authorities about the comet or not tell them? Martin Boes felt sure that he would agree to tell them. He looked out the elevator at Greater Los Angeles. It was a beautiful clear day with no smog. He exited the elevator and found Stilmaker's room. The door was slightly open. He could smell a sweet cigar smoke coming from the room. He knocked on the door and entered, and there was Professor Stilmaker, deep in thought, looking out the window over Los Angeles, smoking his cigar. "Professor?" said Martin Boes. Without turning around, Stilmaker said "Don't tell 'em."

# CHAPTER 4

## Bren's Thing with the Garden Gnome

WHEN JIMBO GOT home, he hugged and kissed his wife, Bren. He was dog tired from working ten hours at *Inland Northwest Shed and Storage*. He was building sheds all day long. Business was good, but work was hard, even for Jimbo, who had been with the job for more than ten years. He switched on the country music station, cracked open a cold one, loosened his belt and plopped down into the Oxblood leather La-Z-Boy. "What's cooking Doc?" he said to Bren in a *Bugs Bunny* manner. "We got leftover spaghetti or leftover beefsteak with Baby Reds, take your pick."

"Mmmm, leftover spaghetti, let's have that. Ever notice how leftover spaghetti tastes better?"

"Yup, and easier to cook up, too." She popped a plate of spaghetti into the microwave, setting it on three minutes. "So!" asked Jimbo, How was *your* day?"

"Pretty good. Worked in the garden a little, and finally met our new neighbors."

"Which ones?"

"The ones across the street in the red-brick two-story. The one with the garden that's better than ours."

"Oh? What's wrong with *our* garden? You're out there every day, working on it."

"The guy's a maniac! He works day and night! He does have better roses. His are up and blooming, while ours are just buds sitting there."

"Oh! You mean that little guy? I've seen him. I thought he was a Garden Gnome, but then he moved." Bren lost it. She busted up laughing so hard, she dropped the dish of grated Parmesan she was holding. The cheese went everywhere. "You! You … are *so right*! *aheeheeheeheehee!* He *does* look like a Garden Gnome! *heeheeheeheeheehee! Hahahahaha!*" She wheezed with true laughter. "With that red hat he wears…*aheeheeheeheehee!*" Jimbo smiled. "You liked that, huh?"She looked at him and continued laughing harder, her laughs trailing off into suppressed wheezes. Tears rolled down her red cheeks. She just couldn't stop. Jimbo was pleased. She didn't laugh like this very often. He wanted to keep it going. *"Nasty Hobbitses stole our precious!"* he said in the voice of Gollum from the *Lord of the Rings* movies. Bren erupted with a new round of laughter. Her face was all red and she found it hard to catch her breath. *"Will you stop?"* she pleaded, chuckling off. She looked at him. He gave her his 'stupid' smile and she cracked up again. "Stop it, you're killing me, she gasped between *heeheehees*. Bren finally caught her breath and stopped laughing so hard. "Geez", said Jimbo. "Maybe I should be a comedian. That's it! I'll become a stand-up comedian. That'll be my ticket out of this rat race I'm stuck in."

"Well" exhaled Bren, back to normal now. "This is one Garden Gnome you might want to know. He's got a '64 Corvette Stingray, Candy Apple Red". She snorted for effect. Jimbo stopped smiling. "What? *You're shittin' me!*"

"Nope. And your Garden Gnome took me for a ride in it today."

"Don't talk about my best friend that way! He what?"

"You idiot!" She took the spaghetti out of the microwave.

Some of the Parmesan was still on the counter, so she put some on the plate. Jim came into the kitchen. "Are you having an affair with the Garden Gnome?" he asked in a mock-serious tone. This of course provoked another round of laughter from Bren. This time she was ready. "Well, at least *he* touches me! — I'm sorry, I just couldn't help myself... a Garden Gnome with a classic 'Vette... and it's in primo condition, too!" Now they were both cracking up. "You bastard... his mother was there, too", she said, punching him on the arm. Jimbo grabbed her, held her in his arms, kissed her and squeezing her soft, supple, pliant ass. "Was she a gnome, too? Let's get to know this Garden Gnome. Invite him and his mother over for Hearts. Maybe he'll sell me his Sting Ray. He's too small for it, anyway, heheheh"

"Good luck on that. And if you say Garden Gnome one more time, I'll tell him you called him that."

"You wouldn't dare." Jimbo plopped back down into the leather easy chair. "I would. I will."

"No you won't."

"Yes, I will."

"I doubt it."

"Try me. See if I don't.""You won't. Know why? Because I'll just tell him you 'bout had a heart attack laughing about it."

"So? You're still the one who called him... that name."

"What name?" He grinned. "Called him what? What did I call him?"

"Please stop." She steeled her lips. He grinned. "Oh! I think it started with a G. I think both words started with a G but the second 'G' is silent...

*Gar* something..."

"*Shut up!*"

"Gar-den Geh-nom-eh?"

"Okay, that's it, I'm telling him!" She got up and made as

if she was going out the door to go tell him. "OK, OK, OK, I'm sorry, I'll stop saying it. So what's his name?"

*"Puddin' tame.* Ask me again and I'll tell you the same."

"What? Come on, what's his name?"

"I'm not gonna tell you, now!"

"Oh, come on!"

"You can ask him yourself, funny boy!"

"Oh, man, don't make me do that!" Bren started laughing again, thinking about the Garden Gnome. "I'll tell you later."

"Oh, fine. Where's that spaghetti? Wait, I'll get it, I can see *you're* not able…"


A week later, Jimbo and Bren had the Garden Gnome and his Mother over for dinner. They all had lasagna and garlic bread with pasta. The garden Gnome's name really was Jerry. He was a Vietnam Vet who had a metal plate placed in his skull, due to mortar fire during warfare. He was still very smart. But, he had a difficult time with his speech. He also worked a lot. Worked all the time. Worked when it wasn't necessary. Worked too much. Made a lot of noise. Swore out loud at imagined foes. Yelled out swear words. Acted crazy. But when he was confronted, he would calm down. He was reasonable.

Bren was interested about the Garden Gnome's garden. She asked him about the proper care of roses, which the Garden Gnome politely gave her with his growing tips. "Your garden is perfect!" said Bren, smiling brightly. "I mean, it's just complete. Your roses are perfect. Your arrangement is sublime. Your bird feeders are the center of attraction in the neighborhood.

"I know the one thing that you need in your garden", said Jimbo. "A Garden Gnome!" There was an audile *ngh!* from Jimbo as Bren kicked his shin under the table.

# CHAPTER 5

## Soleil

THERE WAS NOBODY like Soleil. She was one of the most beautiful women God ever created. Her dark eyes were perfect in every way. Everyone was hypnotized upon meeting Soleil. Everyone was stunned by her beauty. The most wolfish playboys, cavalier rakes and lounge lizards were reduced to stammering schoolboys when confronted with Soleil. The womanizers were shot down before they could even get off the runway. She was sought after by Kings, Princes, and Sheiks. Soleil's eyes penetrated your pretenses, brought you back to reality. She could hypnotize a person into agreeing with her. She could tell what kind of person you were in ten seconds. She was magical. Her thick, long, dark hair was like glossy, spun silk. Her hair was so desirable that she was paid handsomely to model in major shampoo commercials. Her skin was naturally tan, with a healthy cedar glow that one would usually see in color magazine ads. The Sun was kind to her; thus the name *Soleil*. Her body was exquisite. Her skin was unblemished. Her waist was small and curved. Her breasts were pleasingly large, and perfectly shaped. The guys all drooled when she wore a sweater. She could have been a model. Occasionally, she did model.

She was no dummy. She was a degreed scholar and an extremely talented fashion and Interior designer. She was an acute businessperson. She studied Psychology. She was extremely confident, lived alone, single and loved it. The times she did venture out to parties, she always ended up the life of them. Men vied for her affections like Scarlett O'Hara in *Gone with the Wind*. She was smart, witty, but kind. She was very nice to everyone she met. She smiled to everyone, even dogs. She always said thank you and made her friends and acquaintances feel important. She never asked for anything for herself, but was generous to a fault with total strangers. She was a naturally positive thinker, and had learned how to use this to attract the good things in life. She would never hurt a fly, though she broke a thousand hearts. And, she had a dark cruel and thoughtless side, an animal side that was rarely seen.

She was the sometimes-girlfriend of Martin Boes. Martin Boes had hired her to run *Boes-Soleil School of Design*, which was right next door to *Martin Boes Aerodynamics*. But that didn't mean that she was the property of Martin Boes. He had to take his chances with her, like all the other guys. She didn't need his money. She did like him most of all, though. They were almost boyfriend and girlfriend. They still had not slept together, both believing in marriage. There was an applied assumption that they were to be engaged, but Martin Boes had not produced a ring of sorts, yet, and Soleil had never pushed for one. And Martin Boes could live without Soleil, too, if it came down to it, though he thanked God daily for finding Soleil. He was quite a bit older than Soleil, but Soleil possessed an older soul in a young and dazzling body. If Martin Boes was ever going to marry again, it would be to Soleil.

# CHAPTER 6

## Red Diary

**A** YEAR BEFORE THE comet came, Jimbo got home early on Wednesday. He took a half-day off from work after tweaking a nerve in his back. He could do that. He had worked at Inland Northwest Shed and Storage for more than ten years now, and he was "Bubba" there, meaning if he needed to take off, it was all right. They loved him at Inland Northwest Shed and Storage. Jimbo got in, exhaled with a *'whoooosh'*. Nobody was home. The kids were in school. Bren was out doing something. Jimbo grabbed a bottle of *Red Stripe* beer from the fridge. He got three aspirins, turned on the Country Music station, and *whumphed* down into his easy chair. He threw down the three aspirins and washed them down with a big gulp of beer. He kicked back and shut his eyes. The music was fine. Jimbo loved country music, Bren did too. Josh did, too. Jodie sort of liked it, but now she was into her own teenage music. To Jimbo and Bren, country music stood for God and America and for family values and fun and good times, as well as a positive, upbeat look at things. Jimbo listened to a few songs and began to doze off. He lightly snored. Jimbo *snorked* and woke up. He looked at his watch. He had been asleep for an hour. He had to take a pee. He entered the Immaculate Bathroom, tracking mud on the pristine floors. He noted the blue water in the toilet, and started to pee. While he peed, he noticed a small red leather book on the doily atop the toilet. It was Jodie's diary. She must have been writing in one of her early morning reigns in the Immaculate Bathroom. He flushed the toilet, and while washing his hands he noticed that the red leather clasp lock of the diary was undone. She must have dashed off to school and left it there, he thought. He toweled off, and went back to his easy chair.

Jimbo sank back into his easy chair. His back tweak still hurt. He thought about Jodie. He didn't really see much of her lately, in fact for a long time. He'd see her at dinner time on weekends and on Sundays. He'd see her out the door with her friends, like that dorky looking Harold kid. Harold, that was his name. Sometimes he would see Jodie and Harold come up from the downstairs den, where they used the computer for school work. Jimbo looked at his watch. It was 12:30. Jodie wouldn't be home from school until four o'clock. Jimbo got up, went back to the bathroom and looked at the Red diary on the doily on top of the toilet. He remembered the exact position it was in before picking it up and taking it back to his easy chair. Jimbo sank back into his easy chair with his daughter Jodie's personal diary. He didn't feel bad about looking at it, because she had left it just sitting there in the bathroom, unlocked. She should've been more careful. It was a pretty thing. It was made of real bound red leather with gold trim and gilded page edges, and had the attractive gold locket and clasp. Jimbo flipped through the super-thin, yet sturdy pages of Jodie's diary. He was a little surprised at the penmanship of his daughter's scrawl. It was actually very good cursive. She had learned *that* at school, at least, he thought. Jimbo flipped to an early entry:

*"Feb. 5ᵗʰ… I can't believe how Harold and I started making out, we never did that before!"* "Whoa!" thought Jimbo. "Here

we go!" He was a little surprised that she was playing around with Harold, who he remembered as awkward and dorky. He had a sleepy-eyed, hang dog kind of face. He was just ordinary looking, body-wise, kind of doughy... not at all like the All-American athlete she said she liked. Jimbo skipped ahead a little. *March 9th... Harold was all over my boobs today... he was a madman! I must say, his enthusiasm is a turn-on...what is it with guys and boobs? They're just fat!"* Jimbo chuckled. He remembered that one of his teen dates had asked the same question. *March 30th Harold and I were really hot today getting really hard to resist going all the way..."* Jimbo was surprised. He had no idea what was going on down there in the basement. *April 6th... I caught Harold flirting with Cindy, he can go to hell! We only made out for half an hour today..."*

"Uh-oh, trouble in Paradise!" thought Jimbo, smiling. He skipped ahead. *"April 14th... That is it for Harold; I never want to see his ass again! We broke up today if he wants that blond bitch Cindy, he can have her..."* Jimbo admired his girl for not putting up with shit. She was just like him. *"April 18... Harold keeps calling me but I won't talk to him. I hope he's happy with the bitch, now..."*

"That's my girl! Be tough!" said Jimbo. *April 23... Back with Harold again... we really got hot today... nobody makes me feel like Harold does... hope we don't break up again..."* Jimbo felt old feelings return that he had not felt in years. He mused about his high school girlfriends, his own early make-out sessions. He drifted into nostalgia for a minute, and then continued. *May 9th... Harold and I were REALLY REALLY HOT today! He is so good! We were this far from going all the way... my parents will kill us if they find out... Harold is so hard! All I have to do is touch him and he gets rock hard... I can't help myself..."*

"OK, this is getting to be too much now!" thought Jimbo. He didn't want to end up with a pregnant teenage daughter. He read on. Jodie's entries were becoming more and more elicit. He read through the months of the *he put his thing*s, the *he wanted me to*s, the *I never did that before*s, the *I let him do it*s, the *he was so hard*s, the *he touched me there*s, the *he wouldn't do that*s, the *I let him do that*s, and finally, *"December 10$^{th}$... It happened. Harold and I went all the way today! He was just too much... I couldn't help myself, him either. Guess he's my boyfriend now! Dad's going to kill both of us if I get pregnant..."*

Jimbo snapped out of his reverie. His face burned. He looked at the make-out timeline. *They'd been at it for almost a year*! He had no idea this was going on. Bren was going to hear about this, even if it meant revealing he had peeked at her personal diary. This was too much. At the same time, Jimbo was impressed with his daughter's writing skills and the way she described her make-out sessions. Her story-telling sent Jimbo back to that early time in his own life, when he was enjoying sex for the first time She was clearly in charge of Harold, directing him and instructing him on what to do. She orchestrated maneuvers he himself never thought of, and carried them out. But this was way too much. This had to stop. Bren was going to hear about it. It was about this time that Jimbo heard a car pull up out front. He looked at the clock. 3:45! God! He was so wrapped up in his daughter's diary that he forgot about her coming home from school! Jimbo lurched out of the chair, tweaking his sore back again. *"OWWWW!"* He stumbled upstairs to the Immaculate Bathroom and put the Red diary back on the doily topped toilet in the exact position he remembered it lying in. Then, he went to the bedroom and tried to lie down and go to sleep. He couldn't.

# CHAPTER 7

## Doomsayer

**D**ON'T TELL 'EM what?" said Martin Boes. Stilmaker was staring out the window smoking in cigar, deep in thought. He turned around and looked at Martin Boes, squinting."Telly?"

"No, it's me, Martin Boes." Stilmaker still squinted. "Marty! By Gah, you look exactly like your Dad!" He shambled over."*Come to my arms, my beamish boy!*" Stilmaker threw out his gangly arms and embraced the son of his old friend. He whapped him hard on the back with his big paw. Martin Boes flinched from the pain. "*Oof*—yes, I hath slain the Jabberwock!"

"Ha-ha!" said Stilmaker, happy that Martin Boes remembered the *Alice in Wonderland* references they used to toss back and forth. Stilmaker held him with his arms staring at him. "Gah! You look so much like your father!"

"I know, I know. I get that a lot." It was true. All of Martin Boes' descendants resembled each other throughout history. There were portraits going back to the fifteenth century. The family resemblance was instantly recognizable in all of them. "You said don't tell 'em… don't tell 'em what?"

"Don't tell 'em the comet is going to smash into the Earth."

"So, you saw the script?"

"Yes sir, I did."

"You saw that the Boes-Stilmaker Comet was going to hit Earth?"

"It might. It might not. It's still a year away. Too early to tell."

"My figures show it hitting. Over and over."

"My figures show it hitting, but maybe missing. And my figures are better than yours."

"So, we shouldn't tell 'em?"

"No, we shouldn't. I won't tell 'em. You won't tell 'em."

"Why?" Martin Boes knew why, he just wanted to hear Stilmaker say it. "You know why. Because of panic and chaos, and the breakdown of society."

"I still think we should tell 'em."

"Tell 'em what? *'Doomsday is coming, folks, grab onto your seats?'* I think you know better than that." Martin Boes played Devil's Advocate. "Regardless, I still think we should tell 'em. Give people a chance to get out from under."

"Where would they go? This rock is nine miles wide. It's a *planet-killer*. If it hits, there's nothing we could possibly do about it. Think of the dinosaurs, 65 million years ago when that comet hit the Yucatan peninsula."

"I thought that was an asteroid." Stilmaker shrugged. "Some say it was an asteroid, some say it was a comet. I believe it was a comet. There's a fuzzy distinction between asteroids and comets, but not so fuzzy when struck by one. At any rate, there was no escape. Half the world species was instantly wiped out, and the dinosaurs eventually died off. It's official, you know. That's what killed the dinosaurs."

Martin Boes knew Stilmaker was right, but kept it up, just to hear Stilmaker speak. He was a great story-teller. His book about the extinction of the dinosaurs was a New York

Times Best Seller. "I still think we should tell 'em!" Stilmaker squinted at Martin Boes, and then took a draw on his cigar. He stood awhile in uffish thought. "Do you know what would happen if you told people the end of the world was coming?"

"No, what?" He knew. Stilmaker knew he knew.

"It would be the end of the world as we know it. Business As Usual would collapse. Bills would no longer be paid. Mortgages would not be paid. Rents would not be paid. The system would collapse. Anarchy would ensue. Murder, death, riots, looting, destruction, everything! I know you know that."

"Well, isn't somebody else going to see it coming, anyway?"

"That's right! They will. So, let *them* be the Doomsayers, not you. Bad enough you have your name on the comet."

"Your name is on it, too." Stilmaker stopped, exhaled a cloud of smoke. "I never wanted my name on the damn thing! Your father insisted on that over my objections. He went to talk directly to the Man Who Names Comets, and he had the name hyphenated. I didn't want my name on the comet. I take no responsibility for it! Do you know what the name Stilmaker translates to? Beer wagon! Would you be interested in the *"Beer wagon Comet?"* Stilmaker snorked. "But didn't you actually discover the comet first?"

"Yes I did, but only moments before your father did. We were at the same place at the same time."

"What happens when CBAT tells the President?"

"Let 'em. Then, *they'll* be the doomsayers. The Powers That Be will handle the situation. They'll deny the whole thing, cover it up, and *down the rabbit hole they will go!*"

"They will?"

"Oh, sure. If it's going to hit us, there's nothing we can do about it, so why cause mass panic?

Besides, it might miss us. You don't wanna be the *Boy Who Cried Wolf,* do you?"

"No."

"I thought not. My advice is to sit tight. Wait and see what happens. Let someone else find the comet. Let *them* report it. We both could be wrong about our figures, or the comet might bump into something in a year's time. No need to be *Chicken Little* at this time. Besides, I think it'll miss us."

"So we don't say anything?"

"We don't say anything. That way, it won't be a lie."

"It won't be a lie."

"Agreed?" Stilmaker held out his washboard hand. Martin Boes grabbed hold of it and shook. "Agreed... but with reservations."

"Fine, fine. You hungry? Let's go to Cantor's, my treat. I feel like a Pastrami on rye!"

That night at 4:30 AM, the phone rang at Professor Stilmaker's house. Stilmaker and his wife Bambi were nestled in their deluxe feather bed. Grumbling, Stilmaker got up and answered the phone in the other room. It was Martin Boes "I still think we should tell 'em."

"Gah! What time is it?" Bambi heard her husband's deep voice mutter things like *"You'll do no such thing!" "Don't be an idiot..." "Why would you want to do such a thing?" "Will you quit your worrying?" "No, you won't!..."* and *"We'll talk about it later..."* before hanging up. Stilmaker returned to the bedroom, with a "Gah!" as he came in. "What was *that* all about?' asked Bambi. "Eh? Oh nothing, just the end of the world as we know it!"

*"Again?"*

# CHAPTER 8

## Fun and Sex with Precious Metals

MARTIN BOES' SON Rickey lived in, and was caretaker of, his father's house on the ocean in Malibu, California. Rickey was a wild and free spirit. He was a young and restless twenty-four year-old. He was nothing like his father, except for looking just like him. Beyond that, he was not much of a chip off the old block. But he was a killer with the ladies. He never had to ask a girl out all his life. He only had to make himself present at certain occasions, and women would come up to him. They were all attracted to him like a magnet. He was great at all the games and sports. He was a handsome, hard-drinking, life-loving, two fisted maverick. He could do whatever he wanted, whenever he wanted. He was rich, but women were naturally attracted to him, with no knowledge of his potential wealth. Rickey would often put on his cowboy hat and drive down PCH to the local bars and lounges and carry on like any other hick. He was great at Karaoke, and even did some fine boot-scootin' as he sang. The women were all over him like mosquitoes. He always brought someone back home

Rickey pulled up to the beach house in his red Mustang with his new conquest aboard, a busty young blonde. They were both smashed, laughing, tripping and falling, all over each other. They went into the house, straight into the bedroom and had wild, abandoned sex on satin bed sheets. They had a great time. Afterwards, they watched a movie on DVD in Ultra-Def 3-D. They had to wear their 3-D glasses. The movie they were watching was a comedy called *The Return of the Victorians.* In the movie, aliens from outer space come to Earth, landing in Sussex, England in a space ship disguised as a Victorian mansion. They looked just like earthlings except that their skin was pale-yellow colored. But the people didn't seem to notice it— after all, it was Sussex. The alien's only knowledge of Earth was derived from Victorian history, literature and arts. The dressed, spoke, ate, had sex (in 3-D), in a Victorian manner. Their morals were outwardly stern, proper and civilized, but inwardly they were guilt-stricken depraved beasts, just like the real Victorians were. The aliens living in the space mansion portrayed popular Victorian Era characters, like Sherlock Holmes, Captain Ahab, Martin Chuzzlewit, Little Dorrit and more. The people in Sussex became enamored, and fascinated by the New Victorians, as they were called. They wanted to become like them. Soon Sussex was filled up with New Victorians, with their manners and morals. But problems arose with the alien portrayers of Jack the Ripper and Bill Sykes, who took their roles literally, and the New Victorians had to return to their planet, leaving behind the tearful Sussex inhabitants, who were very sad about their departure, but whose lives were nonetheless enriched by the experience.

But the underlying morality tale was lost on Rickey and his girlfriend, who weren't really watching the movie anyway. They were too busy smooching and making out to notice. They did notice opening scene where the Victorian mansion lands on Earth with a gigantic CGI umbrella, and the Ultra-Def 3-D sex scenes, but that was about it. "Hey, I'm dyslexic, how about a Joe Blob?" chuckled Rickey. "What?"

"A Joe Blob"

"What's that?"

"A Joe Blob... I'm dyslexic, get it? I get things backwards."

"I don't get it— Oh! Now I get it!" she giggled. "I don't do things like that on the first date!"

"It was just a joke. You hungry?"

"Yeah."

"Let's get some chow." He picked up a phone. "Hullo, Farnsworthy? Sorry to bother you, could you bring us up a plate of barbecue ribs and some champagne and whiskey and Coca-Cola? Also some Pyrat Rum if there's any... thanks, bye."

"Wow, room service!"

"Oh well, you know... it's good to be king..."

"So where's your Dad?"

"Hmm? Oh, he's in Arizona. I kinda watch the place when he's not around. Don't you worry; he won't get mad at us for using his bedroom." They watched a bit more of the movie. There was a knock on the door "Come in!" yelled Rickey. In came old Farnsworthy, pushing a service cart with a huge platter of barbecued ribs, some whiskey, some Pyrat Rum, some Pimms, an ice bucket with two champagne bottles and a 2 liter of Coke. "Young Mus' Richard?"

"Yes! Thank you so much, Farns!" Farnsworthy looked at the girl, then back at Rickey. "Mus' Richard! I dunnamany times I told 'ee not to use the Master's room...ye knoo he forbids 'ee from doing so!" Rickey grabbed his wallet and pressed a $100 dollar bill into his hand. "Mus' Richard is most generous!" Farnsworthy winked, smiled and left. "Is that your butler? Wow! *You even have an English butler*! How old is he?"

"I don't know 96 or something— that was Farnsworthy. He's been around for as long as I can remember. Let's eat. Here ya go." He tossed her a messy barbecue rib. She caught it, looking at Rickey. "Here's some napkins." He tossed her some napkins, grabbed a rib and they both started eating and drinking. Outside, there was a full moon reflecting off the ocean on Malibu Beach, with waves washing up and over jagged rocks. Shorebirds called. Two hours later, they were both smashed again, laughing, drinking and watching an old B&W movie on the wide-screen. "This is an awesome place, Rickey!" She noticed the secured closet door." What's in there?"

"None of your beeswax, nosey!" He chuckled, got up, unlocked and slid open the door, revealing rows and rows of thousands of silver dollars meticulously stacked in place. They appeared to be placed in molded metal sleeves.

Martin Boes attracted silver to himself all his life. He was a silver magnet, like his son was a female magnet. Telemon Ajax Boes was a silver magnet, too. He discovered several silver mines in Nevada, including one real big one, one that he had hidden the traces of so well, that he could never find it again. He gave his son a map of where he thought it was on his death bed. Martin Boes found it again. He amassed thousands of silver dollars. He left them to his son. Martin Boes amassed even more silver dollars by buying out old silver dollars from Las Vegas casinos, before the price of silver shot up. He had a priceless collection of rare gold and silver coins in the closet. He even had a 1964 silver Peace dollar. In 1963, President Johnson wanted to bring back the old Peace dollars for use in Las Vegas casinos. He ordered 300,000 new 1964 Peace dollars to be minted. Shortly after, the U.S. mint decided not to use silver in the nation's coinage any more. After all, silver was a precious metal. The 300,000 minted silver dollars were melted down. But some say some of the dollars escaped the meltdown. Some say President Johnson got one. Some say Howard Hughes got one. Some say Martin Boes got one, left to him by his father, Telemon Ajax Boes. If he did, he never said so, because it was highly illegal to possess such a coin. "Oh my God! Where did you get all those coins?" said the girl, dazzled. "They're Dad's. He collected 'em over the years. He got most of 'em from Vegas casinos as loan collateral. They stopped using Silver dollars in the 60's and they had 'em stored away. Dad got 'em." She got up and marveled at the stacks and stacks of silver. "You wanna have some fun?" he said. "Hell, yeah!"

"Okay, but you gotta get naked, first!"

"I will if you will!" She started stripping, making strip music sounds "Da da da-da, de da dah…"

"I will, you betcha!" He drank from the bottle. "Now you lay down!"

"What're ya gonna do, ya pervert?" she said, with languid torpidity. "We're gonna be rolling in the dough! He grabbed handfuls of silver dollars and showered them all over the naked girl, who screamed with delight. He laughed and grabbed some more silver dollars and showered them over her. She rolled around the bed lewdly like an early Madonna video, some of the coins sticking to her naked body. He grabbed the bottle and drank, then grabs armfuls of silver dollars. She put a silver dollar over each of her pink nipples, hiding them. "Look, Rickey! Look at my pastries!" He guffawed and took out the champagne bottles from the ice bucket "I think you mean *pasties*— but I like your pastries, too!" He kissed her breasts and then filled up the ice bucket with armloads of silver dollars, shaking it like a mixer. "How about some cold, hard cash, honey?" He threw both the ice and silver dollars all over her. She shrieked as the ice and silver hit her. "Dammit, you bastard!" She threw handful of coins and ice at him, and he ducked back, laughing. "Why Judas! Doncha' want your blood money?"

"What? Who's Judas?"

"Judas… you know… he betrayed Jesus for thirty pieces of silver."

"He did?—I don't get it."

"Never mind, it was just a little Bible humor."

"Oh."

Rickey turned around and dropped two more armfuls

of silver dollars on the bed, and with a rebel yell leapt onto the bed. An orgy of nude sex, silver dollars and ice cubes ensued, with coins flashing and clinking with that distinctive silver sound. There was lots of rolling around naked and fun with precious metals. Coins were placed here, there and everywhere. He put two dollars in his eye sockets, and she pushed in her nipples with a couple dollars. He buried her completely with silver dollars on the bed. They drank and spilled more booze. Coins were everywhere. He fashioned a Silver dollar bikini on her body. She made a Knight's silver dollar armor mesh on his. They fooled around and carried on like life-loving young people do. "Can I use your bathroom?" she asked. "Sure, right over there" She got up and walked toward the bathroom and the silver dollars she had placed between her buttocks dropped out, clinking to the floor. He lost it. "PAHAHAHAHAHAHAHAHA!" The lit cigarette fell from his lips. "Thought you'd like that." she said." "Get over here, you nasty girl!"

"Oh, you gonna spank me?"

"Let your other boyfriend do that. Hey! How about that Joe Blob?"

"What? Oh!—*you men!*" She giggled and jockeyed for position to give him the Joe Blob. As they went at it, The girl stopped for a moment. "Do you smell something burning?" He sniffed. "Oh Jesus! The bed's on fire!" He grabbed the 2 liter of Coke and shook it, then sprayed it on the small fire, putting it out. He tore off the burnt, soaked bed sheet and threw it down. "Now, where were we?" They started having sex again, and right in the middle of it, Martin Boes walked in.

Martin Boes surveyed the scene. It was a spectacle. It was a modern day Roman Orgy. All his silver dollars where strewn about everywhere, blanketing Rickey and his girl. Booze was spilled everywhere, and there were chewed up barbecued ribs on the floor with the burnt satin bed sheets. They were both so drunk, it took them a while to even notice that Martin Boes was standing there looking at them with a dour face recalling Gilbert Stuart's Washington portrait. Finally, Rickey saw him. He froze. The girl looked up at Rickey and then saw his father. She froze. Everybody froze for about an eight count, looking at each other. "Hi, Dad!" Martin Boes walked around, surveying the mess. "Thanks for not breaking open the rare Morgans."

"That's right! I didn't do *that*, did I? I was thinkin' about you all the time, Dad!" Martin Boes picked up a silver dollar. "Uh-huh... so you thought about me, eh? I guess I should be *dumb-ass grateful!*" He flipped the coin. The girl got dressed, furtively stashing some silver dollars away. "Oh, Dad! This is my new girlfriend, Justine— Justine, meet my Dad." Martin Boes smiled sweetly at Justine. "How do you do! Are you really, officially, his girlfriend? You don't know how lucky you are to have that title!" Still drunk, Justine got up, pulling on her blouse. "Well, guess I better get going— I'll call a taxi" She stumbled toward the door, but was pre-empted by Martin Boes. "Ahem" He held out his hand. "Huh? Oh!" She reached into her bra and pulled out a handful of silver dollars, which she put in his hand. "Justine! What the *hell?*" said Rickey, smiling. "Well, gotta go!" She headed out, but he stopped her again, this time holding his hand near her mouth. "Hmm?" she said. He gave her a stern look. She gave him a naughty little girl look, then spat out three silver dollars, clinking them one by one, into his hand. "I *really* gotta go now! 'Bye Rickey! Nice to meet you, Mr. Boes!" She headed out again and he stopped her once more, his palm out. "You're jingling. I hear the sound of precious metals." Justine sighed. "Okay, Okay, Okay, here you go" She reached into her panties and pulled out a few Morgans. "*Justine!*" gasped Ricky, amazed. Martin Boes withdrew his hand. "On second thought, tell you what—you can keep *those*." Justine squealed with delight. "Thank you honey! Bye, Rickey!" And out the door she went. "Bye, Justine! See you around!" Martin Boes now turned to Rickey, still naked on the bed with bottle in hand, silver dollars everywhere, a drunken mess. "Ummm… Hi, Dad! You weren't supposed to come home yet. What's up?" He hiccupped. "Sorry to interrupt your little *soiree*. Far be it from me to ruin your good time" said his father. Nice looking blonde this time. A little slow on the uptake…" He flipped the coin, over and over, tensely. Suddenly, he wheeled around angrily to his good-for-nothing son. "I told you *twice* before not to do this again! And, to stay out of my room!"

"Aw, come on, Dad! What am I supposed to do, give you a warning? You have such great stuff in here!" He made a horse-like *plplplplp* noise, trying to shake off his drunkenness. Martin Boes stared, unmoved. He finally spoke."I should shoot you, like a lame horse… put you out of your misery."

"What horse? What the hell are you talking about, Dad?"

"I'm talking about *you!* I ought to shoot you and put you out of *my* misery!"

"Huh? Good one, Dad! I deserve it. Well, there's the gun over there, go ahead and shoot me!"

"Don't tempt me— I could probably do it and get away with it, too!"

"All right, all right! I'm sorry, Dad, and I promise not to do it again."

"Right. And I bet you have some ocean-front properties in New Orleans you'd like to sell me."

"No, look, I—" Rickey got up, stubbing his toe on the bed leg. "OW, DAMMIT!" He fell back onto the bed, moaning in pain. Martin Boes smiled. "That's what you get when you're *bad*."

"Okay, look, I'm sorry I got a little carried away, lemme clean up this money."

"Don't trouble yourself—" Martin Boes flicked a switch on the inside of the closet. Nothing happened for a few seconds, then lights flashed and a high-pitched alarm sounded. A few silver coins jiggled and started to move, standing on edge!

Soon all followed, coming to life, standing up on their edges at attention. He pressed another button as Rickey stared in awe. The coins swiveled and then flew up and into the closet to their respective places where Rickey had taken them off the shelf, all the coins flipping and flying back up into neatly stacked rows, as before. When all were back in place, he adroitly shut the door and locked it with a key, giving Rickey a knowing glance. "HOOO-WHEEEEEEEEEEEE!"

"You like that, eh?"

"Oh my God, Dad! That was awesome, man! How did you do that?"

"Let's just call it my money management system. Now *you* can clean up the rest of this mess. *And stay out of my room!*"

# CHAPTER 9

## Designed by Martin Boes

ARTIN BOES AND Soleil gave Stilmaker the Grand Tour of the Boes-Soleil main office. It was huge. It was at least 500 feet from end to end and 200 feet wide. It was dotted with strategically placed furniture, terraces and indoor gazebos designed by Martin Boes. The lighting was mostly skylight, with solar powered lighting at night. The windows were made of Ice That Wouldn't Melt, created and designed by Martin Boes.

The room was trussed by giant symmetrical pylons and columns designed by Martin Boes. The pylons and columns were cleverly disguised as rain forest trees with fern gardens and soothing, cascading rock waterfalls designed by Martin Boes. In various spots were ice sculptures made out of the Ice That Wouldn't Melt on refrigerated glass pedestals designed by Martin Boes. In the center of the room was a stainless steel clear beveled-glass spiral staircase going downstairs only, designed by Martin Boes. It was the only way in and out of the main office. To exit the building, one had to take the stainless steel clear beveled-glass elevator designed by Martin Boes down to the revolutionary, award winning employee parking lot designed by Martin Boes. "Professor Stilmaker!" said Soleil, "We wanted to show you this tree." Stilmaker walked over with Martin Boes and Soleil to one of the fern pylons. There was a very small tree in an exalted pottery vase designed by Martin Boes. It sat upon a stainless steel and clear beveled glass plant stand designed by Martin Boes. Stilmaker peered at the tree, unimpressed. "That's...very nice." said Stilmaker. "What kind of tree is it?"

"You've never heard of a Bonsai tree?" said Soleil. "They're miniature trees cultivated for years by the Japanese. This one's five hundred years old."

"You've gotta be kidding me!" blurted Stilmaker. "That's five hundred years old?"

"At least five hundred years old." said Martin Boes. "It's Marty's" said Soleil. "The cost was atrocious. Look at this one." She walked over to another fern-pylon and pointed to another little tree. "This one is only a hundred and fifty. It's a baby. It's mine. Marty gave it to me for my birthday."

"Uh-oh… not again!", said Martin Boes. He rolled his eyes. "Yeah, he wouldn't buy me a five-hundred-year-old one, so I had to settle for this, the cheap son of a bitch!" There was a pause, and then they all burst out laughing. Soleil rarely swore.

They moved on with the tour. Soleil showed Stilmaker the Dodo feather that Martin Boes had acquired from the British Museum. It was encased in a small, beveled crystal case designed by Martin Boes, upon a beveled glass pedestal with an Ice That Wouldn't Melt top designed by Martin Boes. Stilmaker was impressed. He also wanted to see the first Perpetual Motion Machine, designed by Martin Boes. In the center of the office, surrounded by a lush fern arrangement, was the first Perpetual Motion Machine. Actually it was the second one, a copy of the original designed by Martin Boes. The original was locked up for safe keeping, as was The Car That Ran on Nothing, designed by Martin Boes. Martin Boes created The Car That Ran on Nothing- the Ultimate Green Car- by using the same precepts from his Perpetual Motion Machine. There it was! The first Perpetual Motion Machine. Stilmaker peered with amazement. "By Gah, Marty, you're a wizard! How did you do it?" He lit up one of his big stinkers. Smoking was forbidden in Martin Boes Aerodynamics, but Martin Boes allowed his father's friend to do so, unhindered. Martin Boes liked a cigar himself, sometimes. "Oh a little this, a little that— it uses Boesite, that stuff that Dad discovered, remember?"

"How does it work?" Martin Boes thought. "It's hard to explain. Buy my book, it tells how I did it" Stilmaker chuckled. "I see you haven't forgotten how to make a buck!" He *whapped* Martin Boes again on the back with his big banjo hand. "Let's go have lunch! My treat! I heard you had a nice little Bistro on the premises."

"*Oof!*—That, I do— you're welcome to tag along, Soleil."

"No thanks, I gotta get back to design. I'll let you two slug it out. Talk about the old days. I'll catch up with you later. Goodbye, Professor Stilmaker!" She gave him a warm hug. "Goodbye, *Honey*!" waved Stilmaker, smiling sweetly. Martin Boes gave a little *Yikes*! expression and waited for the tempest. He could see the flash of anger in her eyes, but then she smiled and didn't say anything about it, again for Professor Stilmaker's sake.

Martin Boes and Stilmaker took their seats at the *Boes Soleil Café*. Stilmaker ordered a half sandwich and split pea soup, his favorite. Martin Boes had some Shrimp Scampi and a salad. Martin Boes looked brooding and thoughtful. "She hates to be called "Honey" said Martin Boes. "What? Is that why she threw me that look? Heh. What, are you afraid of her or something?"

"Frankly, yes. She slapped me hard once for saying it."

"Good God! What a hellcat. Hasn't she got more important things to worry about?"

"You can ask her, if you want to."

"No, I don't think so… but then again, it might be nice to be slapped by *her*." Martin Boes sat down in his chair, venting a deep sigh. "What's the matter, are you still worried about that comet?" asked Stilmaker. "Yes, of course I am. I haven't been able to get a full night's sleep since we ran those scripts. How about you?"

"I must admit, I have lost some sleep over it from you calling me up in the middle of the night about it. But I'm learning to just accept it. If it hits us, that's it."

"Did you say that the Yucatan collision was an asteroid or comet? The one that killed the dinosaurs?" Martin Boes knew about that, he just wanted to hear Stilmaker in storytelling mode. "I think it was a comet. Some say it was an asteroid. But, that was the cause of the Cretaceous-Tertiary, or "KT" extinction 65 million years ago. There's no other explanation. It wiped out more than half of all species on the planet and led to the extinction of the dinosaurs. The dinosaurs had ruled the world for 160 million years! Can you imagine it? Humans have only been around for about five million. The great lizards might have survived until now, if it weren't for that 9 mile wide comet crashing down in Mexico. The impact was thought to have been with a force a billion times more powerful than the atomic bomb at Hiroshima. The crater was 100 miles wide." Stilmaker tucked his napkin in. "But the final nail in the coffin for the dinosaurs came when blasted material flew into the atmosphere, shrouding the planet in darkness, causing a global winter that killed off many of the species that couldn't adapt. *The poor souls! The poor creatures*! They wandered about in shock, color-blind. They couldn't see their usual prey anymore. They had to use their sense of smell and hearing to find food. Their marine and ecosystems were destroyed, the great lizards languished away, becoming smaller and smaller as the larger ones died out. Half of the mammals were wiped out too, but it paved the way for humans to become the dominant species on earth. Now it looks like *our* turn to become extinct!"

"Please, don't put it that way!" laughed Martin Boes."I'm not ready to go yet!" The waitress brought Stilmaker his split-pea soup. Stilmaker grabbed a packet of crackers and crushed them effortlessly in his big fist. He opened the packet and sprinkled the crumbs into his soup. "Comets are like cats 'he said. "They both have tails, and both do what they want to do." He grimaced. "I was just thinking… this is one cat tail I am worried about."

"What? Why"

"Even if the comet misses Earth, I'm worried about the tail."

"The tail?"

"Yes, the tail of the comet. I'm worried about what could happen with the tail. The world will most certainly become engulfed by the tail of the comet. That's what I'm worried about."

"Why?"

"Because there's a tremendous amount of dust and gas in a comet's tail. There may be some kind of atmospheric disaster."

"So? At least it wouldn't hit us, right?" Stilmaker looked at Martin Boes levelly. "The Yucatan comet hit the Earth, that's true. All of the comet dust in the tail plowed into Earth, too, and blotted out the sun. I'm afraid the tail of the comet, even if the comet misses Earth, will do some kind of damage. Not unlike the dinosaurs. I'm just guessing, but it might result in an atmospheric disaster of some kind. I'm not sure. It never happened before. My figures show the comet missing, but it may change its mind and hit us. We'll see. It's still a year away, something may change."

"I sure wish you and Dad hadn't discovered that comet. I'd feel a lot better not knowing about it."

"How on earth would you never know about it? Well, it's

too late, now. Try to look at it this way. Comets are leftovers of the creation of the solar system. Comets are also like… little galactic sperms. Comets contain life-bearing minerals and chemicals. Comets are part of the ingredients of life on Earth." Stilmaker sipped some soup. He looked at the soup. *"Primordial soup!* That's how life on Earth was said to have started. By a comet crashing into Earth, creating Primordial soup!"

# CHAPTER 10

## Recipe for Primordial Soup

PRIMORDIAL SOUP

**YOU WILL NEED:**

*One 300 Trillion gallon saucepan*
*One Medium Sized Comet\**
*21/2 Tsp. Anti-Matter*
*200 Trillion gals. Water*
*100,000,000 Cups Sea Salt (Non- Iodized)*
*One large mountain of Brimstone (crushed)*

\*A forty-acre square block of chicken bouillon may be substituted, if Comet is not available.

**DIRECTIONS**: In large saucepan add water, slowly stirring in salt, Anti-matter and crushed Brimstone. Bring to boil, stirring often. Toss in Comet, reduce heat to **LOW**. Cover with lid and simmer for One Eon, stirring often. **DO NOT OVERCOOK**. Turn **OFF** heat when done. **CAUTION: HOT**! Let stand 50,000 years before serving. Add salt, pepper to taste. Serves billions. Serving suggestion: Roasted Garlic Triscuit with Pimento spread.

# CHAPTER 11

## I Planted a Thought in a Magnetic Field

EWU WAS DONE spear fishing for the day. He strung the one fish he managed to spear over his shoulder and walked by the ocean, searching for Abalones. He snagged a few of them, putting them in his seal skin bag. He also looked for Jade and Moonstones to trade for food and clothing during the cold months. He found strange things in the ocean tide. One time, he found a small dinosaur skull. He did not know what kind of creature it was. It was like stone, and had rock inside the skull. He took it home and showed the other natives, who were amazed at how the bone was solid rock. Everybody held Ewu in high esteem after he showed them the mysterious skull, which he had decorated and placed in a prominent place in his grass lodge.

Ewu was searching the shore line for Abalones, and he saw some strange rocks that he had never seen before. They were flat metallic rocks with metal nodes stuck on the surface. Ewu kicked one over, flipping the node side down. The flat rock hovered, wobbling a few inches above the ground. Ewu accidently kicked it again, and the flat rock scooted away very quickly, hovering above the ground, and finally stopped as it wedged into a sand bar. Ewu went to the sand bar and pulled out the flat rock. He held it in his hands and stared at it. He had no concept of metal. It was the hardest rock he had ever found. He held it up to his face. When he did, he heard a high pitched ringing in his ears. It stopped when he lowered it. It seemed to vibrate in his hand. He threw it, node side down, and this time the rock skipped across the ground like a flat stone skipping across a lake. Except it was ground. The rock kept going, going, going until it hit a tree and stopped. It landed node side up. Ewu went back to the place where he found the first rock, and gathered up the other strange rocks. Some were floating, some were not. He put them in his hide bag and headed home to show the others.

When Ewu showed the others his discovery, they were amazed, but scared. How could rocks float? Why were they so hard? Who put those nodes on them and why? They were afraid that they might be evil, might be bad medicine. Then, Ewu demonstrated how the rocks skipped across the ground and didn't stop until they ran into something. They all joined in the rock-skipping sport. The kids were very entertained, and asked for some of the rocks. Ewu wouldn't give them away. He wanted them. He told the others where he found them, and that there may be some more there, maybe not. Ewu took the stones home to his grass lodge and showed his wife and children. He placed the biggest rock next to the dinosaur skull. Then he took a few smaller ones and laid down on his bed to examine them in comfort. His wife lit the fire and made supper. The kids went to play in the last light of day. Ewu looked hard at the rocks. He found that they could be chipped with his tools, but only with great effort. He thought about making spears and arrow tips out of the rocks. He held them up close to his face. He could still hear that strange ringing sound as he held them up. He put the rock node side down and watched it hover a few inches above the earth. He pressed it down, and it sprang up again. He bounced the flat rock up and down, as if it were a rubber ball. He pressed it down and held it. After ten seconds he felt a vibration again. He lifted up his hand and the rock sprang up again, floating on air. He felt dizzy. He was tired. He was nodding off, holding up the magical rocks. He put the rocks down near his head and fell asleep. His wife came in and asked him if he wanted to eat, but he was out like a light, snoring. She smiled, and closing the flap, she let Ewu sleep.

When Ewu woke up early next morning, he couldn't remember anything. He couldn't remember his name, or who he was. He didn't recognize his wife and kids, or any of his neighbors. He couldn't recognize his own mother and father. He didn't know how to talk. He had no memory of recent or past events. All he could do was stare blankly, unable to speak, unable to convey his thoughts and feelings. The medicine man looked at his head to see if he was injured, but found nothing wrong. The medicine man said he had a stroke of the brain, which had happened before, but usually with the elder folks. Ewu could see and hear fine, but he couldn't speak. He was reduced to an animal. He recognized fire and danger and felt fear. He was mostly confused. He could walk, but unsteadily, and he couldn't run. His wife was devastated. She had lost her Ewu, though he was still there. He stared dumbly at her and his kids. She made Ewu's bed and found the magical rocks near where he had laid them by his head. She picked them up and looked at them closely. She heard a humming sound in her head and felt dizzy. She never liked the magical rocks. She thought they were evil. She thought the magical rocks had somehow done this bad thing to Ewu, and she was correct. She took the rocks down from the shelf and also took the rock dinosaur skull, which might be evil, too. She took all the rocks and the skull and put them in Ewu's hide bag. She went out to the cliffs and threw the bag into the ocean. She went back home and hugged and comforted poor Ewu. As time passed,

Ewu learned how to speak again, and most of his memory eventually returned. But it took years.

---

Eight hundred years later, Telemon Ajax Boes, father of Martin Boes, was prospecting for gold and silver near the camp where Ewu and his tribe dwelled .He seemed to attract precious metals like a magnet. He'd find gold or silver every time he went out looking. He was also interested in native artifacts. He was always easily finding spears and arrowheads. He had the knack for picking out the really old stuff, no matter what it was. He was a geologist and astronomer. He would eventually discover, at the same time as Professor Stilmaker, the comet that would eventually be named the Boes-Stilmaker comet. He would drive up and down the coast, stopping at intervals for hamburgers and beer. He would search for fossils and precious metal deposits or anything interesting that he could sell to the museums and universities. He always took along his red wagon to cart his findings around in.

On this day, he was walking by the sand cliffs that were previously overlooking the ocean, which was now one mile away. His trained eye saw a skull shaped something sticking out of the cliffs. Most people would never have seen it, but he saw it right away. He got out his tools and began chipping away. It didn't take long for him to see it was a small dinosaur skull. He easily pulled it out from the sandstone, which was loose. It looked like it was partially wrapped in hide which had mostly rotted away. As he pulled the skull out of the cliff, some black rocks fell out and dropped to his feet. One of the rocks floated a few inches above the ground.

Telemon Ajax Boes was startled by this. He had never seen this before. He looked at the wobbling flat rock. It was metallic, and had silver nodes on one side. He touched it with his toe, and it moved away a bit, still floating. He picked it up and looked at it closely. He thought he heard a ringing in his ears when he held it up to his eyes. He flipped it over and looked at the octahedral nodes. It looked like a common nickel-iron meteorite, except for the strange nodes. Meteorites were worth money, so he dropped them in the cart to take home. When he dropped the rocks into the wagon, it suddenly jolted forward. He reached and grabbed it before it got far. *"What the...?"* He held the wagon and turned the rocks over flat side down, and let go of the wagon. It stayed put. Curious, he turned the rocks node side down and let go of the wagon. It shot away as if it had a life of its own. He ran after it. It went fast up the inclined road and slowed down when high on the incline, stopping near the top of the hill. It didn't slide back. He got to the wagon and turned it around and let go. It shot back downhill, even faster than before, slamming into a tree. The rocks fell out and floated there, near the overturned wagon. He caught up with the wagon and picked up the rocks. He put them flat side down in the wagon and went back to the place where he found the dinosaur skull. He found a few more chunks of the meteorites and placed them carefully in the wagon. He examined the petrified rock dinosaur skull. It seemed to have painted colors and *glyphs*, as if someone had decorated it long, long ago. He wrapped it carefully in cloth, put it in the wagon, and lead the wagon back to the F-15 like an excited little boy.

Telemon Ajax Boes got home and told his wife about the great finds he had made. (Martin Boes was not yet born.) He stayed up late examining the skull and the meteorites. The rocks were neutral on one side yet hyper-magnetic on the other side. They seemed to repel the Earth's magnetic field. He put the rocks node side down and called his wife to come look at them. She came in and saw the floating rocks wobbling and spinning an inch or two above the table. She gasped in wide-eyed amazement. "What the..?"

"That's what I said when I found them. They're from outer space and they're hyper-magnetic. They pushed the wagon on their own power... I don't know how. Look at this!" He showed her the painted dinosaur skull. "Wow! What kind of critter is that?"

"It's a small dinosaur. Prehistoric Indians painted it, see?" She looked close. As she got close to the rocks, she heard a distinct hum in her ears. "What's that noise?"

"Oh, you noticed, too! It's coming from those meteorites." He picked up a rock and held it up to his ears. He heard the hum and felt slightly euphoric. "Where did you ever find them, honey?" He sat motionless, listening to the hum and smiling. "Honey? Honey? Are you there?" She put her hand on his shoulder. He snapped out of his trance. "Hmmm?"

"I said where did you find them?"

"Find? I... I'm, uh... *I found them*... I ... They were..."

"Yes?"

"I found them. I found them at the... I ... *I don't know!*"

"You mean, you can't remember where you found them?"

"Of course I know where I found them!" he said angrily. Do you think I'm an idiot?"

"No. I don't. So, where did you find them?" He sighed. "I know where I found them! They were... they were at the... *I can't remember!*" He looked at his wife fearfully. "Am I having a stroke?"

"Do you want me to call the doctor?"

"No, no, I feel all right, I just can't recall where I found these things!"

"I think there's something wrong with those rocks you found. You were just in some kind of trance, listening to them."

"I was not! What do you mean? Oh, I found these rocks and the skull together in the side of a cliff. But why did I forget that?"

She laughed. You must be getting old!"

"I'm only thirty-one."

"You'd better be careful with those rocks, Honey!"

---

Meteorites are formed as condensation products from the gaseous nebula around the Sun and are the primitive materials for the formation of planets, such as Earth. The primary source of all the rocks and minerals-as well as the atmosphere and hydrosphere-on the Earth are meteorites and our Sun, from which all these materials were derived.

Telemon Ajax Boes used all his geological books, tools and knowledge to analyze the strange rocks. They were indeed meteorites. They were *Stony Irons*, made of mostly nickel-iron, pyrrhotite and magnetite- a highly powerful magnetite, a lodestone so powerful that they were very dangerous. The rocks were so hyper-magnetic, they could separate molecules. They were *diamagnetic*, repelling the Earth's magnetic field. They were magneto-polar, maintaining its magnetism for long periods of time- maybe permanently. He placed the floating rocks in an external magnetic field with other metallic minerals containing iron, and they quickly became hyper-magnetic, also. He was very careful not to handle them too long or put them too close to his head. The hyper-magnetism would erase memory.

Telemon Ajax Boes sent a small chunk of the rocks to the International Union of Geological Sciences for analyzing. The scientists were perplexed by the rocks. They had never seen such a thing before. They named the exciting new discovery after its discoverer, labeling it *Boesite*. They asked him where he had discovered it, but he would not reveal where. He remembered how the Boesite pushed his wagon when he put them inside. He had a thought. He fashioned a small cart vehicle out of wood and attached refined Boesite bars underneath the rear wheels of the cart and added brakes. He sat in the cart and released the brakes. The cart jolted out, flipping him in a somersault onto the ground as it took off. It kept going, faster and faster until it hit a wall and stopped. Sorely, he chased the cart down and realized he needed slow release brakes and a helmet. It was powerful stuff, this Boesite. He remodeled the cart with seat belts and slow-release brakes. He got in the cart, strapped himself down in his football helmet and released the brakes. The cart moved out slowly and then went faster and faster. It went so fast that when he tried to turn, he rolled it, breaking his arm in the process. He adjusted the brakes to slow it down on turns. He strapped himself in and this time, it worked! The cart would go faster and faster until he applied the brakes. It took turns beautifully, and he never rolled it again.

He was very excited! He had created *a vehicle that would run on nothing.* He made a runway track just for his new vehicle. He jokingly referred to it as the *Magna Carta*. He called the newspapers and invited them to his demonstration of the Car that Ran on Nothing. The crowd gathered that fateful day in May to see it, with all the media there, news cameras ready, as well as friends and family. He waved at the crowd in his jumpsuit and football helmet and strapped himself down into the cart. He assumed a forward position and pulled the switch, releasing the brakes. Nothing happened. He looked ridiculous, sitting there, waiting to go. The cameras flashed. Laughter erupted. He reassumed the position and pulled the switch again. Nothing happened. The cameras flashed. It would not move. He got out, looked under the rear wheels at the Boesite bars. It looked OK. "Okay, this time for sure!" he said, chuckling embarrassedly. He got back in, strapped himself down, reassumed the position and pulled the lever. Nothing happened. People roared with laughter. The newsmen all made jokes about the car that ran on nothing, to the effect that it did indeed run on nothing, because *nothing happened.* The newspapers had a field day, a holiday with this one, the front page showing the ridiculous Telemon Ajax Boes in his starting position in the non-moving car. The ridiculed him and his so-called Magna Carta.

Telemon Ajax Boes was never more embarrassed in all his life. Even his wife ridiculed him. He could not figure out why his cart wouldn't run, even though it had performed so well when he was by himself. He examined the Boesite bars, and they were still as powerful as ever. He went over it again and again. He put it aside and tried it again two weeks later. He pulled the lever and the cart took off! He studied the differences between his first success, his failure and the second success and determined that the Boesite bars worked on the Earth's magnetic field only sometimes. It worked only when the moon and tidal phases were at a certain point and would not work when that point passed. The car that ran on nothing worked, but it was not practical because it only worked *sometimes*. He went back to the site where he found the rocks to get more of them. He combed the area with a magnet on a stick. He found a few of them, but nothing more. He took them home and made more Boesite from the original rocks into iron bars. He ground them up into silicates and attempted to make a perpetual motion machine from Boesite. He was well paid for his discovery and lived the rest of his life in comfort from his silver mines and investments. He never tried to finish the car that ran on nothing, but left the instructions to his son Martin Boes before he died. Martin Boes finally figured out how to run the car that ran on nothing, years after his father passed away.

# CHAPTER 12

## The Tribunal

THE MARTIN BOES Foundation for Humanity was housed in the Martin Boes Aerodynamics building. Martin Boes personal fortune banked the foundation. Since it was a non-profit foundation, The U.S. Government could not wring a penny in taxes out of it. His crack troops of lawyers set it up so that the Feds couldn't get their hands on his money. In essence, Martin Boes gave away money to people. His money. Martin Boes believed in humanity. He believed that people had the right to exist, to just *be,* without having to be slaves to money. At the same time, he realized the world was all about money, and that people had to work to make a living.

The Martin Boes Foundation for Humanity would provide grants for people in need of money. This was not generally known by the public, and it was not advertised. It was all word of mouth to people. Nevertheless, there was a long waiting list for grants. Anyone could get a grant that would not have to be paid back, for just about any reason. Those who qualified were almost never turned down. Grants could range from two hundred dollars up to fifty thousand dollars, depending on the reason for the grant.

Every Wednesday, Martin Boes would personally give away his money to people at the *Tribunal*. Martin Boes would sit behind a large desk that towered above the applicants. He wore his finest suits. To his right sat Mikey, and to his left sat Soleil. The applicants would enter the Tribunal. Martin Boes would skim over their applications. Then, he would ask a few questions of the applicant. Then, Soleil would ask a few personal questions. Then Mikey, the *ramrod*, would ask a few hard questions, if he had any, and would read the applicant the riot act. A typical Martin Boes Foundation for the Humanities grant session would go something like this:

Victor entered the Tribunal Room under the wing of the ever-watchful Mikey. Mikey led him to a podium facing Martin Boes. Soleil sat at another big desk on the left. Mikey sat down at his big desk on the right. He was armed. Victor stood at the podium while Martin Boes reviewed his application. Finally, he looked down at Victor. "Mister Heerman? Victor Heerman?"

"Yes, your honor. You can call me Victor." Martin Boes chuckled. "Thank you, Victor. I'm not a judge, so you don't have to say your honor. *Sir* will be just fine. And how has life been treating you lately, Victor?"

"Well, Okay, I guess. Could be better."

"I guess that's why you're here today. Now Victor, I understand that you are requesting a grant for ten thousand dollars. I see you have listed your reasons for this money. Now, I would like to hear you say it. Why should the foundation grant you this amount?" Soleil and Mikey looked up from their notepads at Victor. "Well, your honor, I was…"

"*Sir*. Please, sir."

"Sir, I was laid off from my construction job last July. I haven't found steady work since then, what with the rainy weather and all. The mortgage on my house is twelve hundred a month. My savings are all gone. I need dental work badly, and my wife needs to see an eye doctor. She's color blind. The kids need clothes for school. They're about to foreclose on my house. Me and my family have no where to go."

"I see. And why were you laid off from work?"

"Cutbacks. It's been a bad season."

"Yes, I understand that it has been a bad season. What are your chances of your employers recalling you to work?"

"Probably good, but it won't happen until next spring. That's if the weather is good. I keep checking every week, though." Soleil scribbled some notes. "What precisely do you want to do with this money, Victor?"

"Basically get caught up, get a leg up. I'd pay the past due mortgage, fix my teeth, help my wife with her eyesight. Get food and clothing for us all."

"Okay. Are you on any public assistance programs?"

"Do you mean like welfare?"

"Yes, welfare, food stamps, things like that."

"No sir! I want to work. I've never been on welfare in my life. Not even food stamps."

"Very good, Victor. I'm proud of you. I wouldn't disapprove if you were to receive food stamps, because of the kids. That's up to you. But I applaud your work ethic. I wish more people would think like you do. Now, what would you do if the money the foundation granted you ran out?"

"By that time, I should be back to work. I'm trying other jobs too, like technical writing."

"Oh? Are you a writer?"

"Yes sir."

"Really! What do you write about, Victor?"

"I write short stories and articles, besides technical stuff."

"Really? That's great! Do you have any aspirations in becoming a writer?"

"Yes sir. I have two novels done. I self-published one of them."

"And what kind of novel is it, fiction or non-fiction?"

"Fiction. It's a mystery. I only do it as a hobby. I've always dreamed of becoming a famous author. But for right now, it's just a hobby."

"I'd like to check out your novels sometime, Victor. And don't give up on your dream. You can make it happen if you just don't give up. I know it's a tough market for writers out there, but it can be done. People do it all the time. Soleil, do you have any questions for Victor?"

"Yes I do. Hello, Victor, I'm Soleil."

"Hello, Soleil, nice to meet you. I've seen you on TV in commercials. You're very pretty!"

"Why, thank you, Victor! You may not believe it, but I don't get compliments very much. She smiled her winning smile. "How many kids do you have, Victor?"

"Three kids. Two boys and a girl, Kevin, Anthony and Lisa. Kevin's fifteen, Tony's twelve and Lisa is eight."

"I see you've got your hands full. What kind of things do like to do with your kids?"

"We go fishing, the boys like soccer. We go to the park almost every day."

"So, you're a soccer dad, huh?"

"Yep. Mom's a soccer Mom, too."

"And what does Lisa like to do?"

"Lisa likes to write and draw. She's pretty good."

"I think that's great, Victor. I bet she's really smart, too!"

"Smart as a whip. Sometimes too smart for her own good."

"Oh, no doubt! That's part of the package. Now I have just a few more short questions for you. I ask everyone these questions, so please don't take them personally."

"Sure, fire away, *Honey*." Soleil's winning smile suddenly vanished and a stone-cold look of utter contempt replaced it. There was an awkward silence. Martin Boes and Mikey smiled. He had just used the "H" word to Soleil. It was a *big no-no*. She had slapped Martin Boes himself for calling her that, and he was her sometimes boyfriend. The storm abated and Soleil smiled again. "Please don't call me that, Victor. Please call me Soleil."

"I'm sorry, Soleil."

"It's OK, I just don't like that term, myself." Soleil fixed her hypnotic gaze on Victor, that gaze that turned the strongest men into stammering schoolboys, that gaze which *nobody* could lie to. "Now, Victor. Have you ever been in trouble with the law such as felonies or convictions?"

"No."

"Are you fleeing from the law?"

"No."

"Do you or your wife have any drug or alcohol addictions?"

"No. We're social drinkers, that's all. I don't have the stomach for booze."

"Good. Thank you for that. Victor, what is your opinion about your life? How do you cope with your current situation?"

Victor thought for a moment. "I… I'm happy and grateful for my life, so far. I'm happy that we've made it this far. Every day I thank God for the things I do have… my wife, my kids, and a roof over my head… the simple things. I'd sure like to keep 'em!" Soleil was moved. She had a good felling about Victor, now. "Very good. I like your outlook, Victor, and I wish you and your family Good Luck in life. All the best. Thank you. Mike, do you have any questions for Victor?" Victor turned to Mikey, who was poker-faced, as usual. Nobody could tell what Mikey was thinking. "No, I think you've covered everything just fine." Mikey looked to Martin Boes, who spoke. "Thank you, Victor. Will you give us about ten minutes, please, to discuss this? There's coffee and doughnuts outside in the waiting room."

"Thanks!" Victor left the room. "Well! What do you two think? Soleil?"

"I like him. I got good vibes from him. He's not hiding anything. I like his family."

"And of course, you will forgive him for using the "H" word?" Martin Boes gave her a smart-ass look. She looked at him coolly. "Don't push your luck, Mister." He quickly turned to Mikey. "Mike?"

"Seems fine to me. Family man. Hard worker. Salt of the Earth. Checks out good to me."

"All right then. That didn't take long. He seems good to me, too. Do we have all the information on him?" Mikey checked his iPad 5. "Yes sir. We have all the lease info and doctor's statement."

"Thanks, Mike. Thanks Soleil, you both did a great job. We can let him come back in, now. After him, we'll take a twenty minute break and do the next one." Mikey let Victor back in. He had a bit of strawberry icing on his mustache, which Mikey pointed out. He brushed it off and returned to the podium, facing Martin Boes. "Congratulations, Victor! The Foundation has decided to grant your request for ten thousand dollars. It will be awarded to you in two payments of five thousand dollars. This grant money must be spent only for the reasons that you have listed, or it will be forfeited and returned to the foundation. You must provide receipts for all expenditures except for food and clothing. Failure to do so will forfeit the grant and you may be liable for the amount of the grant. And you may not return to the foundation. Do you understand this?"

"Yes, sir, you can count on me."

"Thank you, Victor. Mike will now read you the details of your grant and get your signatures."

"Thank you very much sir!"

"You're very welcome. Mike?" Martin Boes and Soleil left the room. Mikey led Victor over to Soleil's desk. "Please sit down, sir." He sat. Mikey read him the riot act from his iPad 5. "Victor Heerman, you have been awarded the amount of ten thousand dollars from the Martin Boes Foundation for Humanity. You will be awarded in two payments of five thousand dollars each. First payment will be awarded one week from today. The second payment will be awarded in one month from your first payment. You must spend the funds of this grant on the following items only: Mortgage payments, dental costs, optometrist and eye care costs, and food and clothing for your family. You must provide receipts for all expenditures except for food and clothing. Failure to provide receipts will result in forfeit of your award and possible legal action against you. All receipts will be verified. Grantees who have forfeited may face criminal prosecution and will not be allowed future visits to the Martin Boes Foundation for Humanity. Do you understand what I have just read to you, Victor Heerman?"

"Yes sir!" Mikey handed him three printouts of the contract. "Sign here." Victor signed. "And here." Victor signed. "And here." Victor signed. "One more time." He signed again. "Please put your right thumb right here on the iPad and release. Victor pressed his thumb on the iPad, and took it off, leaving a perfect electronic thumbprint. "Congratulations, sir. Your check will arrive via mail in approximately one week. Do you have any questions?"

"None at all, sir."

"Then we are done. Thank you for applying to the Martin Boes Foundation for Humanity. Good luck, sir and have a nice day." They shook hands, and that was that.

# CHAPTER 13

## Jimbo's Talk with Bren About Earthly Matters

SATURDAY, THE GARDEN Gnome was at it again, power mowing his lawn again after only one day. He was noisy as hell. The neighbors complained, but no one wanted to confront the Garden Gnome. He attacked his lawn like a terrier, mowing it too close, its yellow roots showing. He edged it with the edger. He trimmed it with the weed eater. He used the gas powered blower to blow the grass into the streets, where the Garden Gnome's Mom raked it up. All of this was to the tune of his amped-up stereo blasting classic rock. Bren was watching the Garden Gnome when Jimbo came into the kitchen. "Doesn't that Garden Gnome ever quit? He makes so much damn noise!"

"I know." said Bren. "I thought *I* was anal about our lawn and garden. I feel a lot better now."

"I hate to burst your bubble, but I think you should know about your daughter and her study-
date."

"Oh? What should I know?"

"That they're down there in that basement every day, getting' hot and heavy!"

"Oh, I know."

"You… you *know?*"

"Oh, sure. She told me all about it." Jimbo stopped, mouth agape. He blinked. "You mean… you knew about this all the time?"

"Yep." She looked at Jimbo. "How did *you* find out about it?"

"Huh?"

"I said, how did *you* find out about it?"

"Well I… I… I read her diary!"

*"You weren't supposed to see that!"*

"You're damn right about that! But I saw it. She left it open in the upstairs bathroom. Do you know how long this has been going on?"

"About a year."

"Wha? well, why didn't you *tell* me?"

"I didn't want you to get all upset, like you are now. And, because by the time she told me about it, they'd gone pretty far. And I knew you'd be upset. You would've found out sooner or later. Don't worry, they don't go all the way…"

"Oh, yeah? That's not what her little red book says!"

"That's why I also gave them some condoms, just in case."

"You… you *gave them condoms?*"

"Yes."

"Why the hell did you do that?"

"Would you rather that they just go on like that with no guidance, no protection? She's a young woman now, you can't just turn your head and pretend it's not happening. She came to me and asked me about sex with boys. What could I do? I told her the truth."

Josh came into the kitchen. "Dad, can I make a peanut butter and jelly sandwich?"

"Sure, go for it, Tiger." Josh got out the chunky peanut butter, strawberry jam and bread. Jimbo returned to Bren, in hushed tones. "I don't think this kind of humpity-jump stuff should be going on in our basement!"

"You mean about Jodie and Harold?" said Josh, spreading the jam."*You* knew about it, *too?*" said Jimbo, exasperated. "Oh, sure! I caught 'em makin' out lots of times. They do it every day." He ate a gob of peanut butter. "Why the *hell* am I the *last* person on Earth to find out about what's happening in *my family?*" Bren shrugged. "I don't know. I guess things happen that way. It's a delicate situation. Why don't you go play now, Josh?"

"OK" Josh sighed, and took his sandwich and left. Jimbo stood in the same position, adamant. "Well, what are we going to do about this?"

"I'll have a talk with her."

"You're going to put a stop to this, right? What if she's pregnant?"

"I said, I'll talk to her, tell her to be careful. If I tell them to stop, she'll know you saw her diary. Do *you* want her to know that that you were looking at her diary?"

"No, but…"

"She's a pretty level-headed kid. She listens to me. Would you rather have them learn about sex at the schoolyard, or in a car somewhere? Have them act like sex is secret and shameful? It would be really hard to tell them to break up. Do *you* want to break them up?"

"No, but I…"

"I mean, you *are* the head of this house. You're my husband and I love you. You pay the bills and bring home the bacon. I understand how you feel. If you want me to, I'll break them up and Harold won't come over anymore. I'll do it if that's what you want."

"No, you don't have to do that, I—*No! I don't care!* I won't have them doing their humpity-jump stuff in our house! I won't have it! Someone's going to have to put the Fear of God in those two!" Jimbo was mad, but deflated. He trudged back to his easy chair. "Look, just don't let her know I saw her diary, Bren."

"I won't. Don't worry, everything will work out. She's smart as a whip."

"And a damn good writer, too, I might add." Jimbo *whumphed* down in his leather easy chair and exhaled a big sigh. The Garden Gnome started up his noisy gas-powered leaf blower. Jimbo swore quietly under his breath.

---

Jimbo was not through, though. He came home early from work three days later and intercepted Harold as he came over to "study" with Jodie. "Come on in, boy sit on down, tell me about yourself. So you like my daughter, do you now? We think she's something else." He roughly grabbed Harold's shoulder with his powerful hands. He came very close to Harold's face, amiably rubbing his rough, stubbly face against Harold's young and tender face. Harold smelled his sour beer breath. "Yes, sir. I like her a lot."

"Good! She's my little girl and her Momma's world. She deserves respect. That's what she'll get… *ain't it, son?*" Jimbo looked him deeply in the eyes. "Oh, yes sir!" Harold was terrified, certain that Jimbo knew what he and Jodie were doing. "Sit down, son. You wanna beer?"

"Um, I don't…"

"Have a beer! It's the breakfast of champions! Makes ya *strong*!" He slammed the can in front of Harold. Harold took the can and opened it. He never had a beer in his life. "Drink up, son!" Harold took a sip of the bitter-tasting brew. He never liked beer, but drank it, not wanting to displease Jimbo. "So, I hear you're on the football team! What do you play, quarterback?"

"No, I'm second string center, sir."

"Great! You look like a tough boy… let's see what you

got!" Jimbo put up his Popeye arm and elbow on the table to initiate arm-wrestling. Harold obliged, pitting his fresh, smooth elbow and arm against Jimbo's mighty, muscular guns. Jimbo's big hands engulfed Harold's strong but young and tender hand. Jimbo said "OneTwoThreeGo!" and instantly slammed down Harold's arm onto the table, stinging him with pain. "Go again?" They clasped hands again and Jimbo slammed Harold's hand down harder this time. "Come on, son, I know you can do better! Have some beer and try again." Harold took a big gulp as Jimbo watched him. He almost spit it up, but managed to gulp it down. "Ready?" They clasped hands and Jimbo slammed Harold's hand down hard on his knuckles, bruising them badly. "Agh!" said Harold, wincing in pain. "You all right, son? Did I hurt ya? I'm sorry. Here, have another drink. He handed Harold the can. Harold meekly drank up. "I knew you were a tough boy. Of course, I have a few years on you, so that's OK. Come on into the den and I'll show you my gun collection." They got up from the table and Jimbo threw his arm around Harold's shoulder, crushing the teenage boy amiably against his drunken self. Jimbo herded the terrified Harold into the den, showing the boy his hunting rifles. "I killed an elk with that 30-30 and skinned him myself. I shot a bear with that one and cut off his head and claws with that knife... here they are!" He grabbed the bear claws and slapped them into Harold's hand. "You ever gone hunting, boy?"

"N-no sir, I haven't" Jimbo looked at Harold thoughtfully. "Well. Looks like we're gonna have to go hunting some time. Jimbo grabbed Harold by the neck and pulled him close to his beer-sodden face. "Looks like I'm gonna have to teach ya how to hunt". His iron fingers pressed into Harold's soft neck. "I'll show ya how to kill something and then gut and skin 'em. Wouldja like that, son?"

"Huh? Sure!" Harold was petrified. He must have found out about him and Jodie, for sure. "

"We'll have a great time. Oh, didja wanna go study with my daughter, now?"

"Huh? *No!* No, I gotta be going now, tell Jodie I said "Hi". I really gotta go home now."

"Oh that's too bad. I was gonna tell you about the time I shot that bear in Utah. But, I guess if you have to go, you have to go. Here, finish your beer. Waste not, want not." Jimbo stood there smiling, watching Harold swallow down the bitter brew. To Harold, it took forever. Finally, he finished the can. "That's my boy! Well, you take it easy, son. I'll tell Jodie you said "Hi".

"Thank you sir! Well, good bye, sir!"

"Jimbo. Call me Jimbo, son." He held out his powerful paw. Harold took it and Jimbo crushed his already bruised hand like a vise grip. Harold had never had his hand shaken so hard in his life. "Thank you, Jimbo. Goodbye, sir."

"Goodbye, son."

*"What did you say to that boy?"* demanded Bren to Jimbo, sitting in his easy chair, three days later. "He won't even come inside the house now! He stays outside in his car, and Jodie sits outside in the car with him. He won't take a step inside the house anymore! What did you say to him?"

"Oh, nothing. We just had a beer and I showed him my guns, that's all. It's a Daddy thing. I didn't say anything about him and Jody or her diary, I promise you that. Your secret is safe with me."

"Well, it looks like you won't have to worry about them making out in the basement, because he won't even come in now." Jimbo sighed. "Gee, that's too bad. What's for supper?"

# CHAPTER 14

## In the Field Where I Died

**J**USTINE BREATHED HARD, her heart pounding with fear. Martin Boes' son Rickey had a gun and was trying to kill her! Hiding in the laundry room, she tried to listen for the enraged Rickey, but the combination of her beating heart and the pounding surf outside of Martin Boes Malibu beach house prevented her from hearing anything. She knew she had to get out of the single-entrance laundry room, or be a sitting duck. She crept out the door and scooted up the garden path, past Farnsworthy's quarters. "Justine! *Justii-iine!* Where the hell are ya? Will ya quit hiding, I ain't gonna hurt ya!" yelled the drunken Rickey, waving his pistol around. Justine jumped behind the night-blooming Jasmine. *"Come out, come out, wherever you are!"* He shambled down the garden path looking left and right. He sniffed the Jasmine in the air. "I kin smell your perfume, you can't hide your lyin' eyes from me!" He came near to Justine, but she avoided him and hid behind the Jacuzzi. "Hey! *Come on!* This hide and seek shit ain't fair! *Where you at?"* Justine went the other way up to the patio, climbed the stairs, opened the sliding doors to the house and went in.

Rickey couldn't find Justine, so he went back inside the house. Fueled by rage, he was going to kill her for betraying him. He stalked down the main hall gun drawn, turning and turning. He thought he smelled her perfume again, but it was only the bathroom deodorizer. He heard the hallway door open behind him. He whipped around, gun pointed. It was Farnsworthy. "Eh, eh, 'tes Mus' Richard, out on a lark again?" He saw Rickey pointing the gun at him, and frowned. "In yer cups again? I dunnamany times I told ye not te play wi' wippons when yer drunk! 'Ere, now!" Farnsworthy advanced towards Rickey, his ancient, gnarled hand outstretched for the gun. Rickey fired the gun once, hitting old Farnsworthy in the chest. One shot would take care of him. Farnsworthy stood, with an incredulous look on his face. He looked down at his fatal wound, then back at Rickey. "Mus'Richard, ye killed me!" He tottered back and fell, slumping over a secretary, then flat on his back, dead. It was almost theatrical. Rickey looked at Farnsworthy with a slack-jawed gape. "Nice old guy ... didn't want him *dead*, but he got in the way" he muttered. He heard a noise in the living room. "Justine! You can't hide, I know you're in here! He checked his Dad's room, which he was not supposed to go into, but did so, regularly. Not in there. He checked his own room. Not there, either. He went to the main living room. It was dark. He switched on the lights and peered into the living room. He could see Justine trying to hide behind the entertainment center. "I'm here, Justine."Justine came out from behind the wide screen, her arm behind her back. "Don't shoot! Please, don't kill me, Rickey! I'll do anything you want! Oh, God! Don't kill me, Rickey, I love you! Don't you believe me?"

"Nope." His heart was made of steel. "You lied and betrayed me, then almost had me killed!" "I— I don't know what you're talking about!"

"Sure, you do! You remember don't you? That hay field? The field where I died? Turns out I made a remarkable recovery, huh? Now, you're gonna pay me back, you lying bitch!! Paybacks are a bitch, bitch!"

"Don't shoot. They'll catch you and throw you in jail." Rickey snorked. "Heh. I can kill you now right here and nobody'll ever know about it! I'm a *citizen above suspicion of the law.*"

"If you kill me, you won't get this." She reached for her purse and at the same time brought up the gun she had behind her back. But Rickey was too quick and slapped it away, out of her hands "Goodbye, Justine, you were good in the sack but that's about it!" He aimed point blank at Justine, who closed her eyes shut tight. Suddenly, there was gunfire from the doorway. Rickey was hit in the shoulder and the side. The impact caused him to spin around like a rag doll and fall, splayed, onto the floor in front of the wide-screen. Justine looked up and saw who had fired at the doorway. It was Soleil. "Oh God, Soleil, is it you? Thank God! Rickey got drunk and went *nuts!* He was gonna kill me! Oh my God! Thank God, you saved me!"

"I know." Soleil seemed remarkably distant and remote. She walked up to the splayed Rickey on the floor, who was trying to reach his gun. She stepped on his hand and picked up the gun. "Nice shot, Soleil. *God, you're beautiful.*" slurred the mortally wounded Rickey. "Thanks." She stood back up, flipping her long hair back, looking flatly at Justine. Walking over, she helped Justine up. Justine sobbed and collapsed into her arms, tearfully embracing the beauteous Soleil, who rolled her eyes. "Are you all right?"

"I think so— yes" sniffed Justine.

"Good." Soleil fired her gun into Justine's chest. She grabbed her by the waist to keep her from falling, and then sat her down on the floor. *"Why?"* asked Justine. "Because you're worth more dead than alive', answered Soleil, coolly. Justine expired without comment. Soleil turned back to Rickey, who was sitting up. "Damn!" he said "You are one cool kitty! You go 'round killing people often?"

"Only the bad ones." She smiled her winning smile. Even splattered with blood, Soleil was beautiful. "You some kinda bounty hunter?" Soleil appeared lost in thought. Finally she spoke. "You might say that." She picked up Justine's gun. "You said she was worth more dead… does that go for me too?" Soleil smiled. "You don't miss a trick, do you?"

"What? Whatsat? Wadda you mean? C'mon, Soleil call 911, I'm dyin' here!" Soleil regarded him as if he were an eel. "I don't know. Should I kill you?" She pointed the gun at his forehead. Rickey was brave and unafraid. "Hell, I don't care… do what you gotta do— *Honey*." That was it. Rickey had sealed his fate by using the "H' word in reference to Soleil. Soleil was livid with rage. He was a dead man. "You're a dead man! Honey is *bee shit!* Nobody calls me Honey and lives! You die now!" She pointed to fire. "I think not, *Honey!*" Soleil turned to the doorway and there was Martin Boes, holding his AR-15. "If anybody's going to kill my son, it's going to be me!" Soleil wheeled around quickly to fire, but Martin Boes let loose from the hip with a ten-round burst, catching Soleil in the chest, neck and head. She fell dead beautifully, her death grip firing off all the bullets she had intended to fire at Martin Boes. He walked over to Soleil and knelt down, checking her pulse. She was dead. "One thing you should know… *never* call her Honey!"

"Dad! Dad! Thank God you got here in time! These chicks were trying to kill me! They already killed Farns! They're crazy! And her— she's some kind of bounty hunter or paid assassin!" He pointed at Soleil, who was making a *crrrrr* death-rattle. Martin Boes surveyed the bloody mayhem. "It's Okay now. Everything is going to be all right. He put down his rifle and walked over to Soleil's body. "She was my girlfriend, you know."

"Dad, call 911, please!"

"We were going to get married."

"Dad? Dad! Did you hear me? Call 911, I'm hurt bad!"

"What is it that they do to the wounded or lame horses?"

"What? What? What're you talking about, Dad?" Martin Boes was putting on some gloves. He picked up Soleil's pistol and walked over to Rickey "Ah! They *shoot* horses, don't they?"

"Dad! Don't do it! Don't kill me!"

"Well look, son, my girlfriend is dead now because of you. We were going to get married. And I saw Farnsworthy when I came in. He was still alive, and he said *you* killed him. Farnsworthy was in our family for forty-six years. Now he's gone, because of your drunkenness. And if I can't get away with calling Soleil *Honey*, you sure as hell can't, either." He raised the pistol. "Don't shoot. They'll catch you and put you in jail. Think about that!" Martin Boes snorked, just like his son had, minutes earlier. "I told you once before, that I could kill you and get away with it. After all, *we are citizens above suspicion of the law*" Rickey mouthed the familiar litany as he said it. "Besides, they'll think Soleil killed you, with her gun."

"Dad! I'm your son! Don't kill me!"

"You? You're just a no-good punk! Like I said, if anyone is going to kill my son, it'll be me!"

"Dad!" Martin Boes fired, killing Rickey.

---

Martin Boes stood there, counting up figures in his head. Suddenly, he spoke."That's one kill for Soleil, one kill for Rickey, and two kills for me. I win. Game over. You can all get up now! Great job, you guys! Soleil, you were magnificent! Loved the death grip gunfire and the death rattle."

"Did you really like it? I was channeling Angelina Jolie"

"Hon— lady, you put Angelina Jolie to shame!"

"Call me Soleil."

"Soleil, you put Angelina Jolie to shame! And you're much prettier! Did the *Gelpels* sting you?"

"They stung a little bit. So, you think I was convincing?" she said, peeling off her bloody wounds. "Hell yes!" cried Rickey, picking the bullet wound off his forehead. "You scared the shit out of me! It was …like you were another person!"

"Really? Hmm. Maybe I should take that movie offer the Emir made to me." She glanced at Martin Boes. "I smell Oscar!" laughed Justine, rolling her eyes and picking off the "blood" from her blouse. "You do?" said Martin Boes. "Maybe Oscar should take a bath!" There was a pause, and then they all laughed. "Good one, Dad!"

"But seriously, you should." said Martin Boes to Soleil. "You should take the offer from the Emu. You're extremely pretty and very talented. I sure couldn't stop you. Justine, thank you for the great acting, you were very convincing. "Dad! You were more convincing than anyone! You scared the shit out of me!" said Rickey. "Well, I guess that's what role-playing is all about."

"Where did you learn to act?" Soleil asked Martin Boes. "You were terrific!"

"Oh, it was nothing, really. I did a little acting in high school and college, that's about it. I was just ad-libbing, thinking of some bad movie clichés… isn't it funny how the most overused movie clichés still work, still affect people? That's how powerful movies are." Farnsworthy burst through the door. He was peeling off the "blood" from his white sport coat. "Are 'ee done now? 'Tes over, yes?"

"Well done, Farnsworthy! Here's the old trouper! So glad you played along!"

"Me pleasure, to be sure, Sir. 'Tes true. I ha' trod a few boards in me time. And hommany points was my liddle death scene worth?"

"Two-hundred and fifty points, Farns."

"Eh?Eh?, only two-fifty? Did 'ee not say the lady's death were worth three-fifty?"

"Why yes, Farns, but servants are not worth as much as gentry." He looked seriously at Farnsworthy. Farnsworthy looked at him, mouth open. Seconds passed. Martin Boes broke first. "I'm just kidding, Farns! You are definitely worth three-fifty, dead." Farnsworthy guffawed and roared with laughter, along with everyone else. They all peeled off the "blood" from themselves until their clothing was clean and new again.

# CHAPTER 15

## The Ice That Wouldn't Melt

*Reporter: "You are Professor Stilmaker, are you not?"*
*Stilmaker: "You're mistaken. I am."*
*Reporter: "Professor Stilmaker, what is your*
*opinion of Martin Boes' latest invention?"*
*Stilmaker: "Absolutely worthless!"*
*Reporter: "His invention?"*
*Stilmaker: "No, my opinion."*

ALL OF THE windows at Martin Boes Aerodynamics and at Boes-Soleil School of Design were made of *Ice That Wouldn't Melt*. Martin Boes, direct descendant of rich, powerful, and influential sorcerers, alchemists and wizards, whipped up a concoction of mercury and some other gaseous elements into a potion that, when added to water and frozen, became Ice That Wouldn't Melt (ITWM). ITWM ice cubes for drinks worked great, as long as the drink was cold to start with. But that was not all. ITWM was used for sculptures and even window panes. As long as an ITWM object was on a cold base, it would not melt, even at 130 degrees. There were large ITWM sculptures created by world famous artists, strategically placed throughout Martin Boe's spacious offices. They were placed on solar-powered refrigerated bases atop beveled glass pedestals designed by Martin Boes. They would never melt. They were permanent fixtures. ITWM was among Martin Boe's greatest achievements, along with his Perpetual Motion Machine, was the Car That Ran On Nothing, Gelpel, and X-Ray Crayons.

To make ITWM windows, plain water was poured into flat, rectangular plastic molds with refrigerator frames. A small amount of ITWM solution (or *Secret Sauce,* as Martin Boes jokingly referred to it) was added to the water. The molds were then frozen. The molds were removed and the result was ice window panes that were just as good, or better than glass. The framed ice-glass panes were then installed, the refrigerated frames powered by solar panels on the roof. Los Angeles tended to heat up in the summer. The ITWM windows wouldn't melt, even at direct 100 degrees, all day long. Mist sprayers would refresh the windows every 24 hours, or, they could be washed by hand. The ITWM windows and art objects served dual purpose by helping cool things down inside during hot weather.

Martin Boes had successfully patented the Ice That Wouldn't Melt. Others could not figure out the formula for ITWM. The Secret Sauce formula for ITWM was kept deep down in The Vaults, where Martin Boes kept all his secret formulae. If you wanted ITWM, you had to come to Martin Boes. He was now in the process of creating ITWM car windshields. When shattered, the ITWM windows would shatter into harmless chunks of ice instead of sharp glass. He already had them installed on his own personal vehicles. Soleil had one on her red Beamer, and they would also be a standard feature on the future Car that Ran on Nothing. Other automobile manufacturers were changing their windshields over to ITWM. They would eventually become standard for all cars.

Although there was a wall of ice that wouldn't melt between Martin Boes and his ex-wife, it did not hinder his creative genius. One big breakthrough invention by Martin Boes was *Gelpel.* Gelpel was a gelatinous compound contained inside a soft pellet. It was similar to a paintball pellet, but smaller. Gelpel pellets were fired from a simple spring-loaded gun that Martin Boes called the *Zipgun.* The Zipgun fired the Gelpel pellets with great accuracy. When the Gelpel hit its target, it would splat in the shape of bullet holes. But the great thing about Gelpel was that it after it dried, it could be easily peeled off skin and fabric, leaving no stain. They were in movies and TV and were even adopted by the military for war games war games. Gelpel splattered just like bullet holes and stuck, creating realistic red blood "wounds". When they dried, they could easily be peeled off fabric and skin. Goggles or other eye protection should be worn, of course. Another fun thing about the Gelpel Zipgun was that each contained a sound card that produced realistic gunfire from actual recordings.

The first Gelpel gun resembled an ordinary paint gun, but shortly afterward Martin Boes created replicas of famous firearms and rifles. He even made Gelpel Springfield rifles for the Civil War re-enactor industry. Each replica rifle or handgun had a sound card with the authentic report of that rifle. Gelpel caught on like wildfire and revolutionized the paintball industry. It was a tremendous success and created yet another fortune for Martin Boes, modern day Wizard.

Another breakthrough invention by Martin Boes was *X-Ray crayons.* Mixing the hyper-magnetic *Boesite*, uranium and wax, he created a crayon that would separate molecules just wide enough apart so that objects could be seen through. He demonstrated his invention in front of a media audience. He presented it like a magic act, because that's what he was.

*Magical.* From offstage, his bodyguard and right-hand man Mikey made the introduction to the audience.

"Ladies and gentlemen, we now present to you the great and magical astrophysicist, inventor, humanitarian and modern day wizard. Please welcome the legendary Martin Boes!" The audience applauded and Martin Boes came onstage in a magician's satin tuxedo and silk top hat. He took off his hat and bowed to the audience. Placing his hat on a table top side down, he then spoke to the audience.

"Thank you for your kind applause and thank you Mike, for your over-generous introduction. I would like to present to you tonight, my latest invention…" and a rabbit popped out of his hat on the table and looked at him. The audience applauded and laughed at the rabbit, which was unnoticed by Martin Boes. "Thank you again, ladies and gentlemen, you are most kind. I would like to present to you tonight, my latest invention…" and the rabbit squeaked. As Martin Boes looked in the rabbit's direction, the rabbit ducked down into his hat. The audience roared with laughter. "I would like to present to you tonight, my latest invention…" The rabbit popped back up again and squeaked and the audience laughed again. Martin Boes looked and the rabbit ducked back down into the hat. "Excuse me but I don't understand. Is there something funny going on here?" He walked over to the table and picked up the hat, flipping it over and over and looking inside. He held the empty hat high in the air, giving the audience a good look. He shrugged, put the hat back down and returned to the center of the stage. "Ahem…ladies and gentlemen, I would like to present to you tonight, my…" And the rabbit popped out of his hat again and squeaked! The audience roared again. He turned and looked and this time he saw the rabbit. He rolled his eyes. "Ladies and gentlemen, I would like to present to you my assistant, The Beauteous Soleil, who will assist me in removing this rabbit from my hat!" The beauteous Soleil came out, dressed in a stunning, sexy, glittering costume, her long, long dark hair shimmering like silk satin. The audience applauded and whistled at the gorgeous Soleil, who smiled and picked up the rabbit from his hat, bowed, waved and walked offstage. "And now", he continued, "I would like to present to you tonight my latest invention…" he looked over at his hat, making sure the rabbit was gone. More laughter. "But first, I would like to present to you my own money management system. I present to you, the Dancing Dollars!"

Martin Boes held up both hands, turning his empty palms over so the audience could see. He cupped his hands and made an upward tossing motion, and suddenly his cupped hands were full of jingling silver dollars. Applause. "Soleil, if you will?" Soleil came out and took the silver dollars from his hands and went down to the audience, showing them that they were real silver dollars, even letting them pick up some and inspect them. Then she returned to the stage and put the dollars on the table in a pile. Martin Boes clapped his hands and produced a magic wand out of nowhere. He pointed the wand at the dollars and chanted *"Plata est activa!"* and the silver dollars stood upon their edges at attention! Applause from the audience. He motioned with his wand and the dollars swayed left and right in unison. *"Plata est momo!"* he chanted, and the dollars started dancing! They twirled on edge, and rolled around the table in a pas de deux dance, flipping over and over. They wheeled and spun and twirled. Martin Boes walked over and waved his wand back and forth over the dancing dollars. The audience was awe struck. How the hell can he do it? There were no strings, no invisible wires. They continued dancing until he waved his wand over them and chanted *"Plata est inertia!"* The dollars spun on edge, and leaped into stacks of neat, rolled coins on the table. The audience roared with wild applause at the feat as Soleil picked up the dollars and went offstage and presented the silver dollars to some audience members. After the applause died down, Martin Boes spoke.

"Thank you, thank you very much. Well, enough wizardry

for one night. It's time for me to now present to you my latest invention. I assure you, ladies and gentlemen that *this is no trick*. No sleight of hand is involved. No mirrors or rabbits. What you are about to see is *absolutely real*. I now present to you the *X-Ray Crayon!* Soleil?"

The Beauteous Soleil came out carrying an easel with a large tablet of paper on it. She placed it center stage. Martin Boes put on some gloves and walked over to the table and picked up a small metal cylinder. He took off the cap of the cylinder and went over to the easel. He drew a large circle on the tablet and filled it in with the crayon. He tore the sheet off the tablet and held it out to the audience. Soleil then stepped behind the sheet of paper. Her beautiful smiling face could clearly be seen through the paper. The audience applauded. Soleil went backstage and brought out a plank of wood. Martin Boes drew a large circle on the plank and filled it in. Soleil stepped behind it and the audience could see Soleil through the circle drawn on the plank of wood. She smiled and winked and went backstage, returning with a section of drywall and held it out. Martin Boes drew another large circle on it and filled it in. Soleil stepped behind the drywall and a fainter but distinct image of her smiling face could be seen. More applause, then Soleil went backstage and came back with a sheet of steel. Martin Boes drew a circle on the steel and filled it in. Soleil stepped behind it and the audience could see a very faint image of Soleil through the steel sheet. The audience applauded, and Martin Boes said "Thank you, Soleil, for your assistance." The audience applauded and whistled as the Beauteous Soleil, smiled, bowed and left the stage. "Now, ladies and gentlemen do you have any questions about the X-Ray Crayon? Yes sir, you in the second row."

"Can the X-Ray Crayon be used on people?" Martin Boes paused. "Hmmm… that's a good question. Let's find out!" He went over to the table and picked up a small pane of glass. He held it up and drew a circle on the glass, filling it in. He held it over his face, and a clear image of his skull was visible. The audience gasped, and then wildly applauded. He held the glass over his face, removed it and put it back over his face, still revealing his skull. "Thank you very much, ladies and gentlemen" said the talking skull. "This ends our presentation, thank you all so much for coming out tonight." The audience gave him and Soleil a standing ovation as they bowed, saluted and walked off stage.

The X-Ray crayon was not a trick, it was real and worked. But it was not yet practical to use as a replacement for X-Rays, because it was made with *Boesite*. *Boesite* was very dangerous and even deadly if applied directly to human skin. *Boesite* could separate the molecules on skin if left there long enough and it could erase human memory if exposed to the brain too long. The X-Ray crayon had to be encased in lead, and even then, Martin Boes was taking a risk handling it. There was still work to be done to make it safer to use.

# CHAPTER 16

## Hitler's European Vacation

O NE YEAR PASSED, and the coming of the Boes-Stilmaker comet was imminent. It was determined that the Boes-Stilmaker Comet would miss the Earth by a narrow margin. Professor Stilmaker appeared to be correct in his calculations. When the comet arrived, the gravity tug from the Moon would pull the comet out of the Earth's path. But there was always still a chance that the comet might change its mind and *what the hell*, slam into Earth. The comet's orbital projection called for it to come very close to Earth over the Persian Gulf. Iran, Iraq, and Afghanistan would get the best look at the Boes-Stilmaker Comet. As a safety precaution, the President of the United States ordered an immediate evacuation of all remaining military troops and personnel from that area. This dovetailed nicely with his promise of finally ending the war and bringing the troops home! There was no certainty about how close the comet would come, but it would no doubt come closer than any comet in recorded history. The International Space Station was safe from the comet, so the crew was prepared to witness the spectacle and take photos.

In the week before the comet arrived, Martin Boes and

Soleil went on one of their infrequent dates. Soleil suggested a funny movie, something that would take the pressure off of Martin Boes' impending sense of doom. He felt something bad was going to happen with the comet. It was a miracle to get Martin Boes to go to the movies anymore, especially since Audience Interaction was instituted at most movie theaters. Martin Boes disliked the rude people who talked, ate with their mouths open, put their feet up on the seats, all that stuff. It had been years since he had been to the theater. It would take the beauteous Soleil to convince him to go. Even so, Mikey, his big black Bodyguard and right-hand man would chaperone, as he always did. Mikey was always there. Mikey was Martin Boes' driver, bodyguard, security chief, and street-smart connection to the real world. He was also part of The Martin Boes Foundation for Humanity tribunal, which approved loans and grants to qualifying applicants. Martin Boes and Soleil were the other members of the tribunal.

Martin Boes paid the forty dollars admission for two. They sat down in the back near the projector wall, with Mikey sitting two rows behind them on the other side, far enough for privacy but close enough to see Martin Boes with his eagle eyes. They were a little early. Soleil wanted to use the restroom before it started. She asked Martin Boes if he wanted some popcorn or a Coke. "Oh! Some popcorn, please, with no butter on it, just a little salt, um, two sodas and some Dots and whatever you want. Here…" He held out a twenty to Soleil. She looked at it and then looked at him, smiling. "What? What's wrong?" Soleil shrugged. "You don't have enough money. Popcorn's ten dollars, sodas are five dollars and Dots are five dollars."

"What? *Are you kidding me?* Ten dollars for one popcorn? No way!"

"Well, prices have gone up". Soleil was momentarily cruel. "It's been a while, old man!" Martin Boes raised one eyebrow and smiled, looking at Soleil. "Yes, it has. I guess Father Time has caught up with me. He's coming for you too, Soleil, and sooner than you think."

"I'm sorry I said that, Marty… I wasn't thinking."

"It's OK, forget it. Here." He gave Soleil another twenty, smiling sweetly. "I guess I'm just a cheap date— did you want anything?"

"No, I'll just have some of your popcorn. You'll save a fortune on me!"

"It's a little too late for *that!*" Soleil laughed and went to the snack bar. As she waited in line, a man tried to hit on her, as usual. She couldn't go anywhere without that happening. She easily stared him down.

———————————

The movie they were watching was a comedy called *Hitler's European Vacation*. It was set in1944 in a remote Alpine resort, *Motel Sechs*. Hitler was there, incognito. He wanted to get away from all the bad stuff that had been going on lately with the Reich. He drove a Model 1Volkswagon Beetle designed by Porsche. He shaved off his all-too-familiar mustache. One scene took place in the resort's beer garden:

The Oompah-pah band stated playing and a blonde Nazi boy sang a patriotic Reich song, mentioning, purity, the Fatherland and other mottos. Hitler enjoyed a stein of beer and listened. After the song was over, the Oompah-pah band suddenly jumped up with machine guns. They were actually crack troops of the French Resistance. They pointed their weapons in every direction. "Is the coast clear?" said the leader, who got the OK wink from the bosomy beer garden *fraulein* in the dirndl dress. Hitler sat still, not moving. The Oompah-pah band sat down and started playing again. The blonde boy returned up and sang a different tune:

> "*That Hitler guy, boy is he wrong*
> *He's been stinking up the world too long,*

> *We don't want a Thousand Year Reich,*
> *We want someone that we like,*
> *He's very small, with only one ball,*
> *We'll have a whole new Fatherland,*
> *When we get rid of that Nazi man,*
> *On him, we'll answer nature's call,*
> *and send him to Hell in a frying pan!"*

---

Martin Boes reached over and cupped Soleil's big boob in his palm. *It felt so good!* Soleil let him. He pushed in on her boob. Soleil just smiled and kept watching the movie. There he was, Martin Boes: genius inventor, millionaire and philanthropist, copping a feel like a 17 year-old in a drive in. Mikey noticed, smiled and shook his head. He'd seen it before. Martin Boes tried to get under her sweater, but Soleil stopped him. "Mikey's looking", she whispered "Watch the movie!"

---

Hitler sat, mortified. After the song, the Oompah-pah resistance fighters laughed and sat down and had some beer. Half of the people hated Hitler and wanted him dead; the other half didn't know who Hitler or the Nazi's were. Two resistance fighters came and sat down with Hitler. "So! Did you like our new song? I wrote it myself. We're the resistance. We heard Hitler might come up here, so we thought it would be an excellent opportunity to *waste his ass*. We saw a very early model Volkswagen parked at Motel Sechs. We're gonna kill him— you wanna help us out? Say, you look familiar! Were you ever here before?"

"Huh? Oh yes! I've been here many times! I hate that Hitler guy, too. He's a Dictator, you know. He's a bad man, a very bad man!"

"You're darn tootin', he is! Why, if Hitler were here right now, I'd skin him alive and make bratwursts!" He showed off his big sharp knife. "Heh heh... well, I don't think I'd... I mean Hitler would be stupid enough to come here and put himself in danger— Ooh, look at the big *busens* on that girl over there! Well, excuse me I must use the bauhaus... er, the bathroom."

*"Just a minute!"* said one resistance fighter, raising his machine gun. "I really feel like I've seen you somewhere before! What's your name?"

*"My name?* Oh! My name is... Rudolf... Rudolf Schmitler! Why?"

"Hold him!" Two resistance fighters held him down in his chair. The leader reached into his pocket and pulled out a tin of shoe polish. He dabbed a spot of it under Hitler's nose. They stared at him for three minutes. Finally: "Nah, it can't be him. He's too fat."

"Nah, you're right... he'd never come here."

"He'd have to be a total retard to show up here! Hahahahaha!"

"We're sorry. I guess we're seeing Hitler everywhere we turn. That's how against him we are."

"Oh, no problem!" said Hitler "You guys are doing a great job; keep up the good work— now if you'll excuse me." He got up to go to the bathroom and get the hell out of there, but bumped hard into the waiter, who spilled the four steins of beer he was carrying all over him. "Dumbkopf! Scheisskopf! Your moronic idiocy is typical of all non-Aryans! How would you like to end up in a concentration camp, you *Juden?* — Oh! Did I say that? Heheheh. Hey guys, did you like my Hitler impression?"

"Eh... just so-so."

"I've seen better."

"Needs work."

"I'm from Tasmania", said the waiter.

Hilarity ensued. The movie went on, ending with Hitler and Eva Braun narrowly escaping in their very early model Volkswagen Beetle, Hitler promising Eva that things would be fine after they took Stalingrad. Martin Boes and Soleil enjoyed the funny movie, and afterwards Mikey drove them to the Santa Monica Pier. They went to the Fun Zone. They went on the solar-powered, psychedelic, illuminated Ferris wheel. They made out when the wheel stopped at the top for a few minutes. It was one place where Mikey couldn't see them. They all had hot dogs, burgers and fries. Later, Martin Boes and Soleil went for a walk on the beach, with Mikey hovering on the cliffs overhead. They smooched, and started making out, but Soleil cut it short- "Mikey's watching", she reminded. So, they called it an evening and Mikey dropped Soleil off at her apartment and took Martin Boes home.

# CHAPTER 17

## Machinations

OES-SOLEIL SCHEDULED THEIR annual weekend campout to coincide with the arrival of the Boes-Stilmaker Comet. Everybody would get a terrific view from the top of Mount Pinos, in the Santa Monica Mountains above Los Angeles. There was much anticipation throughout the world for this comet, being that it was the closest a comet ever came to earth. Thousands of comet viewing parties were organized and assembled for the event. Promises, wishes, and wedding engagements hung upon the comets arrival. All observatory tickets were sold out. Telescopes and binoculars were all sold out, even though the comet could be clearly seen in detail with the naked eye.

Many canny marketers made millions off of comet mania. There were comet binoculars, comet glasses, comet T-shirts, comet backpacks, comet cameras, comet jackets, comet scale-model kits, comet pens and pencils, comet hairdos, comet viewing chairs, comet cocktails *(Tail o' the Comet)*, comet soft drinks, comet cheeseburgers, comet beer, comet cigars, comet ice cream, comet automobiles, comet candy and gum, comet commemorative coins and stamps, comet books, comet toys and games, comet apparel, and special comet viewing gear, all created for the tremendously anticipated event.

Boes-Soleil scheduled a very special comet viewing party in the mountains above Los Angeles. It was at that time that time when Martin Boes would propose to Soleil and give her a diamond engagement ring. Martin Boes picked up his iPhone 7 to text and invite her to the campout. He was still not quite used to working the new, amazing gadget. For all his genius and inventiveness, he was still old school. He was getting better at learning to "chat". He picked up on the abbreviations and symbols in text messaging, but he was very careful about what he texted to people. Too many kingdoms had toppled because of unfortunately worded text messages. It was not easy for him, because he had used proper grammar and spelling naturally all his life. He now texted Soleil in his usual informal style:

*Hey, you! U R formally invited to the 2nd Annual Boes-Soleil 9 Mile Rock Campout with special viewing party for that comet with my name on it. R U coming? I got my Boy Scout knife and my Boy's Life mags. We're going climbing, too. Would you like to climb mt pinos? RSVP. Cheers, MB"*

Martin Boes pushed SEND. "Your message has been sent" said the iPhone in Soleil's voice. For some strange reason— perhaps through the agency of an ill-natured Fairy— the automatic spell-check on his machine did its job, and slightly misinterpreted the text message he had just sent to Soleil. This was how Soleil would receive it.

*Hey, you! U R formally invited to the 2nd Annual Boes-Soleil 9 Mile Rock Campout with special viewing party for that comet with my name on it. R U coming? I got my Boy Scout knife and my Boy's Life mags. We're going climbing, too. Would you like to climb **my penis?** RSVP. Cheers, MB"*

# CHAPTER 18

## The Emu's Offer

**W**HEN SOLEIL RECEIVED Martin Boe's text message, she couldn't believe her eyes.

*We're going mountain climbing, too. Would you like to climb my penis?* Of all the nerve! She had dated Kings, Princes, Sheiks, and Presidents, and no one- not even the Emu- had ever spoken to her that way before! *Sexting* from Martin Boes? That was the last thing she expected from her shy, ultra-mannered sometimes-boyfriend. She checked the ISP on her phone and made sure it wasn't a mistake. The message was indeed from Martin Boes. *We're going mountain climbing, too. Would you like to climb my penis?* Soleil's face and ears burned with anger. Her sometimes-boyfriend genius inventor, humanitarian and modern day wizard had reduced himself to *sexting*, had lowered himself to a sexist, white trash pig! She thought about it. Who the hell did he think he was, embarrassing her like that? True, she was always teasing him in their make-out sessions, but that didn't mean she was some kind of easy tramp! What's more, Martin Boes *never* talked dirty. Never swore. It wasn't like him at all. She looked hard at the text message. *We're going mountain climbing, too. Would you like to climb my penis?"*

There was no mistake. He meant to say that. What was he thinking? He probably thought he was being clever. People said things in texting that they couldn't say in person, face to face. Still, it was creepy and pathetic, coming from *him*. She toyed with the idea of suing him for sexual harassment. He was her employer. If she wanted to, she could bring Martin Boes crashing down to ruins, just by releasing the text message to the press. It would ruin him, destroy him. She could make millions from the settlement, but she dismissed the idea of a lawsuit because it was well-known that they had a relationship together. Mikey knew about it. The janitor knew. The Emu knew. Everybody knew. She simmered down. They had been going out for two years. They had never had sex yet, though they had gotten awfully close to it. They had a pact, saving it for marriage. They both believed in that. She liked him a lot. He was ripped and handsome, and smart and witty. But he was too reticent. Too polite. Too mannerly. Too stand-offish. It wasn't easy to get him to make out in public places, as she liked to do. Of course, Mikey was always watching, but that was part of the thrill. She considered the Emu.

The Emu was his only real arch-rival for her affection. He had proposed to her several times, and the last time she almost gave in. She could have a life of luxury as his wife, but there would be a price, being herself. The Emu offered to make her a movie star. But the Emu would own her as property. She would be the ultimate trophy wife. No one owned Soleil. And the Emu was a *real* pig. But even he knew that he couldn't get away with saying something like *Would you like to climb my penis?*

It was well-known that Soleil hated to even be called *Honey*. Many had tried, and suffered the consequences. She had actually slapped Martin Boes face for doing so! He thought he could get away with it. He was wrong. No one had the courage to say such a thing to her before. It was as if he *knew* she could ruin him, but didn't care. He was very bold, risking everything, daring her to have sex with him. She smiled. Only Martin Boes would do such a thing. She realized at that moment that this was what she wanted from him, what she was *needing* from him… guts, balls, manliness! Soleil's head swam. She was liking his sext-message now. She was liking him more and more now as she read it. *We're going mountain climbing, too. Would you like to climb my penis?*

She was falling in love. She could feel it. She rarely had that feeling, but she knew she had it now. She bet that he thought she was going to be upset. She'd show him she was game. She'd show him a thing or two. She grabbed her iPhone 7 and punched up a text message reply to Martin Boes:

*"I gladly accept your invitation. Got my Girl Scout knife and handbook. Love camping out under the stars. Can't wait to go climbing, too…Cheers!"* Soleil pushed the reply button. A voice sounding very much like Martin Boes said "Would you like to save this message? Say Yes to save."

"Yes." said Soleil.

# CHAPTER 19

## The Wisdom of Keeping Your Mouth Shut

T HE COMET THEY were making such a fuss about was a life-bearing, dirty ball of gooey ice. It was the stuff life was made of. It contained Carbon, for the most part. It had lots of carbon. It also had hydrogen, oxygen, salt, ammonia, carbon monoxide, deuterium, and who knows what? Along with eclipses, comets have been the most feared and admired sky spectacles of all. But while astronomers have been able to predict eclipses for thousands of years, only in the 1700s was a comet's return correctly predicted, by Edmond Halley.

Hovering in the most fragile of gravitational balances, a fleet of dirty, lumpy snowballs numbering in the trillions is barely held in orbit by the pull of the sun. They are stored in the *Oort* cloud, a huge, diffuse sphere of cometary nuclei in the far reaches of the solar system. Comets are leftovers, scraps of material that didn't make it to planethood in the events creating our solar system. Once, many astronomers believe, the solar system was full of comet nuclei, chunks of ice and dust left over from the formation of the sun. Most clumped together to form planets, leaving a relative handful- averaging perhaps a few miles wide, with temperatures as low as minus

400 degrees Fahrenheit (minus 240 degrees Celsius) as time capsules of the early solar system.

The Boes-Stilmaker comet orbited in a perpetual state of languid torpor until some subtle gravitational nudge upset its delicate balance. Then the great fall began. Imperceptibly at first, the big, gooey snowball drifted toward the sun and steadily accelerated. As solar radiation heated up the comet, the ice within sublimated, escaping as gas from vents at the surface. Sometimes jets of sublimating ice whirled off the rotating comet nucleus like a fireworks pinwheel. Dust trapped in the ice broke free. Pushed back by the pressure of the sun's radiation, the dust streamed out behind the comet in what appeared to be a fiery tail. With each visit to the sun, a comet loses more of its ice. Eventually it would become a rocky ghost, its glory days gone for good.

It has been suggested that each year Earth is bombarded by ten million house-size mini-comets weighing up to forty tons each. Some comets swing around the sun every few years. Others may take thousands of years. Most can be seen only with a telescope. But every once in a while- a few times a century- an impressive one is visible to the naked eye.

Just as Stilmaker said, the wayward Boes-Stilmaker Comet was detected on its collision course with Earth. It was reported to CBAT, who passed it on to NASA, the President and The Powers That Be. The Boes-Stilmaker Comet was going to give Earth the best view of a comet, ever!

The people were told that the comet would be the closest pass to the Earth, ever. There would be a spectacular celestial shower- *"A dazzling display of lights!"* said the Powers That Be. This was a lie. They were not told just *how close* the comet would come. Or that it might hit Earth. Or that the tail of the comet might do something...*that* was covered up. They didn't know for sure what would happen. But they knew one thing for sure. The Powers That Be would not tell the world that it was doomed. That would be worse than the comet smashing into the planet. If everyone knew they were going to die, that would be the *real* end of the world. Panic, chaos and despair would rule. Mortgages would not be paid. Loans would be sloughed off. The Economy would collapse. Anarchy would rule. It would be the end of Business As Usual, just as a nuclear holocaust would mean the end of Business As Usual. The Powers That Be would never actually set off the nukes, because that would mean the end of Business As Usual. The Powers That Be could make such a decision. But this comet-hitting-the-Earth thing— that was beyond their decision-making powers. They couldn't do anything about it.

They couldn't shoot it out of the sky with nuclear missiles-the thing was nine miles wide, traveling at 25,000 miles per hour. Even if they *could* hit it with a barrage of nukes, the radiation would result in billions of billions of pieces of fallout for everyone! It would be much worse than the comet itself. They couldn't possibly land on it. It was going much, much too fast. Even if they could attempt to land, comets are really like *goop*, and not really strong enough to support a space ship. Comets spin and whirl, throwing off ice, dust and life-bearing chemicals as they get closer to the Sun.

Since there was a *fifty-fifty chance* that the Boes-Stilmaker Comet would miss Earth, the Powers That Be saw no reason to declare Doom. The Powers That Be did not want to just pack it in, give up. *Not now.* The comet was predicted to pass close over the Persian Gulf and through Asia. That was the other side of the Earth. The Western Hemisphere would miss it. There would be no kindly, sympathetic but helpless President addressing the nation of impending doom. There would be no doom-saying. No drawing of straws. There would be no panic, fear, disruption of Business As Usual. There would always be the *Chicken Little's*, but they would be disregarded. The Powers That Be took faith in Stilmaker and the other astrophysicists in their scripts calling for the Boes-Stilmaker Comet to *miss* Earth. The Powers That Be had spoken.

There was a knock on Martin Boes' cabin door. It was the night before the comet. The Boes-Soleil Weekend Getaway and Comet Viewing Party were all settled in at Mount Pinos. Everyone had their own tent except Martin Boes, who occupied a rented cabin. His faithful bodyguard Mikey was situated nearby in his own deluxe tent, within view of his cabin. Martin Boes answered the knock at the door. It was Soleil. She wore a big, black Stetson Cowboy hat that he had bought her for the weekend getaway. "Howdy!" said Martin Boes. Howdy, Pardner!" she said, entering the room. She took off the hat and tossed it without looking onto the antique hat rack in the corner of the cabin. "Nice shot!" he said. Soleil tossed her hair lush, silken hair and pushed it to the top of her head, and let it fall, shaking it loose. "Thanks, Skippy! Got anything to drink?" Martin Boes went to the cooler and brought out a bottle of red wine. He smiled at Soleil. "So, did you enjoy our little trek today? I see you got some sun… Soleil."

"That's my name, don't wear it out." Soleil meant *Sun* in French. She was perfectly named. She was indeed a Sun person. The slightest sunlight gave her already perfect complexion a warm, cedar glow. This increased her beauty two-fold making her even more irresistible to men (and women). "I loved the hike. Loved what we did at Crystal Lake, too." She glanced at him, smiling. They had had a torrid make-out session under the waterfall, under Mikey's remote, watchful eyes. ""*Here, shtick on some mewshic!*" she said in a Humphrey Bogart voice. She tossed him a CD. He caught it, chuckling.

"That's a very good Bogart you do, there." He put the CD on. It was the jazz-fusion album *How Could I Stay Angry At You?* by Nina Winchester. He uncorked the wine bottle and poured out two glasses in plastic cups that looked like crystal wine glasses. "You must have saved a fortune on those", smiled Soleil."

"All right, all right, enough with the cheap jokes, already!"

"Sorry, I couldn't resist."

"I know. You never let me get by without pointing out my thriftiness. Besides, how do you think I got rich? It was by watching my money, hon-..." He caught himself just in time. Soleil's dreamy dark eyes momentarily flashed with anger. "You were gonna say the "H" word, weren't you? You know how I hate that. Haven't you learned by now?" She went over to him and ran her fingers through his hair and up and down the veins on his brawny neck. "At least you didn't hit me this time! My, you are frisky today. That tickles. You've been doing that since we got up here." She dragged her mouth down the side of his neck. "I like to do it. It reminds me of a hard co—..." There was a sudden knock on the door. "Who is it?" said Martin Boes.

"It's me, Sir." Said Mikey. The ever-vigilant Mikey checked up on his boss, no matter who was with him. "I just wanted to let you know that the campfire will be ready in two hours. Just to let you know."

"Thanks Mike. We'll be there with weenies and marshmallows. Thanks for the heads up."

"You're welcome." Mikey left. "*I've* been thinking about weenies all day long." said Soleil. "Good God, you *are* in rare form!" he said, with surprise "What brought all this on?"

"Oh, something you said."

"Something I said? What did I say?"

"You know damn well what you said." She gave him a long, lush kiss. He had absolutely no idea what he said. When the kiss ended, he said "Oh, that." She looked at him straight in the eyes.

"You *do* remember what you said to me, don't you?"

"Of course I do!" He had no clue. "I remember everything I say!" He remembered nothing. "I'm very careful about what I say to people, especially you, Soleil." He hadn't the foggiest notion what she was talking about. "I'm so glad you said it. It really turned me on. I wish you'd say things like that more often." She ripped open his shirt, the buttons flying. She pushed him down onto the feather bed. Soleil was in a state of languid torpor. She grabbed the wine bottle and gulped down seven gulps. "This is a side of you I've never seen before. Not that I'm complaining!" he said. "Well, you brought out this side of me. It's all your fault." Soleil sat on top of the prone Martin Boes. "It's kind of warm in here." She took off her sweater, revealing her red satin bra that he liked so much. Her big breasts bulged out of the slightly too small bra. She ran her fingers over the red satin, enticingly. "Hmmm, might as well take this thing off, too." She unhooked her bra and her large, perfectly shaped breasts fell out, bouncing. Martin Boes was in heaven. She had never gone this far with him before. She would always just tease him, play hard to get, which of course, she was. He still had no idea what it was that he said to spur her on this way, but he was smart enough to know when to keep his mouth shut. That was one thing that was passed down from generation to generation in his family. *The Wisdom of Keeping Your Mouth Shut.* Soleil drained the wine bottle and tossed it away. She piled her long, glossy silk hair on top of her head and let it fall. She swayed back and forth on top of him. "So! Are you enjoying the Mountain scenery down there?" She jiggled her breasts enticingly. "Oh, yes! The peaks and valleys… the slopes." She grabbed his hands and put them on her breasts. His fingers sank in, crushing at the intense softness, getting a good feel. She laughed and flipped her long, long hair down over him, drowning him in her lush silkiness. "You can get lost in my hair."

"Mmmmmmm, I love it!" Soleil now went from a state of languid torpor to a state of sex-crazed animal. It had been building up for so long. The *animus* of Soleil was finally released. She devoured him, her fingers digging into his chest and abs. She ground her palms down hard on his hard shoulder muscles, getting a good feel. She laced her fingers through his hair, grabbing it, pulling it. She clawed at his back like a wildcat. She yowled and hissed and moaned very loudly. He winced with pleasure and pain. She started to unbutton his jeans, but Martin Boes said, "Before we go any further, Soleil…does this mean our pact is broken? I mean, about our waiting to get married first?" Soleil gave him a knowing smile. "You don't know when to shut up, do you?"

"I did. I mean, I do. I just wanted to make sure that…"

"Well, *shut up!*"

"Yes Ma'am."

And so it was that Martin Boes and Soleil made love for the first time, brought about by an erroneous spell check in a text message suggesting that she climb his penis.

And so she did. After they made love, they relaxed in each others arms, enjoying the jazz music. Martin Boes figured that she had just finally come around to him and his manliness. He was very cocky now, so to speak, and he felt in charge. He momentarily lost his wisdom of knowing when to keep his mouth shut. "Well, I guess I can call you *Honey* now, right, Honey?" Soleil gave him a sweet smile as she sat up. She put her arms on his shoulders, and then she back-handed him hard in his face. Martin Boes saw stars, Saturns and little tweeting canaries in his field of vision. "Good answer!" Soleil melted into laughter and kissed him. She was in love with him. They went another wild animal round in love-making. Outside in his tent, Mikey could easily hear Soleil's yowling and hissing. He smiled and nodded his head. "About time!" he said. "About *damn* time!"

---

Martin Boes and Soleil took their weenies and marshmallows and went to the campfire. It was a splendid, clear and starry night. All the folks sang traditional campfire songs from their youth. Mikey played guitar while Ikey sang.

Martin Boes and Soleil roasted weenies and marshmallows. Soleil liked to burn her marshmallows black. She said they tasted better that way. Martin Boes tried one. "Hey, you're right! They do taste better burnt. Very good, Soleil!"

"One of my many hidden talents, burning up marshmallows!" They laughed.

"You burned *me* up back in that cabin." he said.

"Hehheh. Didn't expect that, did you?"

"No. And believe me, I'm not complaining."

"Didn't think I'd take you up on your offer, did you?" She looked at him, devilishly. He was about to ask what offer she meant, but changed his mind. He still had no idea what she was talking about. "Nope! But I'm sure glad you did! *Why wait?* that's my motto." They lay back snuggling, looking up at the starry sky. "I wonder if there really is intelligent life up there." Soleil mused. "No." said Martin Boes. "You mean you don't believe in extraterrestrials?"

"Nope."

"Do you mean to say, that out of all the billions of stars and galaxies, you don't believe in intelligent life out there?"

"No, I don't believe so."

"How can you be so sure?"

"I know there is no intelligent life out there, and not very much down here, either!" He smiled. "I'm just kidding. But there is no intelligent life out there."

"In the whole Universe?"

"The whole Universe."

"But what about all the evidence? What about Roswell?" Martin Boes snorked. "There is no evidence. There's no proof of aliens from outer space. Roswell was a hoax that got out of hand and became folklore. It's all just folklore, hallucinations or hoaxes. There was never any solid proof. Not even a good photo or video. You would think with everyone having access to cameras and videos these days, that there would be volumes of photos and film of them. But to this day, there is not. With all the so-called close encounters and alien abductions, there is still not one dead alien found."

"Dead?"

"Yes, dead. If the aliens were here, we would've found a dead one. Same thing with Bigfoot, Sasquatch and the Abominable Snowman. We would've found a dead one. That's because there aren't any. There never were."

"What about the Ancient Aliens theory?"

"It's just that, a theory. A story. A very good story, but just a story. More folklore. Besides, the aliens, if they existed, could never make it to Earth."

"Why not?"

"They would be much too far away. It would take many thousands of years to get here, even if they did manage to build a spacecraft capable of going light speed. Sentient beings cannot live for thousands of years. Maybe moss or lichens or gases, but no living beings."

"What if there really were other worlds out there? There must be!"

"What if? *What if?* What if angels danced on the heads of pins? We'd detect them. If there were any inhabited planets within our galaxy and beyond, we would have detected them. And they'd have to follow the Earth's Laws of Physics. Earth Science isn't perfect, but it's pretty damn good. It's all speculation." Martin Boes pointed up into the clear night sky. "Do you see that big bright star up there? The one that's just off the handle of the big dipper?"

"Yes, I see it" said Soleil. It's twinkling with colors."

"That was Zeta 6. It was a gas giant."

"*Was?*"

"Yes, was. It's not there anymore."

"But, I see it right there!"

"No, it's not there. What you see is the way it looked one million years ago. That gas giant was one million light years away. The light you see took one million years to get here. The star exploded a half a million years ago. You are seeing it before it exploded."

"That's amazing!" Soleil was truly impressed. "I never thought about that." "No one does, unless you're an astronomy geek. You are actually looking back into the past, many thousands of years ago, with your own eyes. Most of the brightest stars you see up there right now are gone. They don't exist anymore."

"That's incredible. It's almost scary."

"Yes, it is. It makes you realize how insignificant we all really are. Light travels at 480,000 miles per hour. Can some being make a spacecraft that could go that fast? Can some being live for a million years, much less a thousand?" He looked at Soleil. "No."

"Then you see what I mean. For all intents and purposes, there are no alien beings out there."

"What about time warps, or folds in space?"

"Again, only speculation. Hawking admits it. Sagan admits it. Sagan thinks there might be aliens, but I don't. It makes for a nice story, though. Unlike the fellow in *The X Files*, I *don't* want to believe."

"Okay, Mulder!" she laughed. "But don't believe me." he said. "Ask any astrophysicist, like Professor Stilmaker. It's all basic stuff."

"Oh, you're no fun at all!" Martin Boes just smiled.

---

The next night, the Boes-Stilmaker Comet came. The viewing party was there with telescopes, binoculars and cameras. Everyone from Boes-Soleil was there, and son Rickey Boes and his new girlfriend Justine showed up. Even old Farnsworthy was there, riding along with Rickey and Justine. He was familiar with comets. He was a small child when Halley's Comet passed by in 1917, and saw it again seventy-six years later. Professor Stilmaker chose to stay at home and watch it with his wife.

Martin Boes sat cuddled next to Soleil. He had certain plans when the comet passed overhead. "Here it comes!" shouted Mikey, and all heads swiveled in unison to the West. There was the Boes-Stimaker Comet, brighter than any star, coming fast. "Aye, do 'ee see it? 'Tes a beauty, 'tes!" exclaimed Farnsworthy, peering through his old spyglass. Because it was passing so close to Earth, the comet only took an hour to pass overhead, instead of days or weeks. All cameras, telescopes and binoculars were raised. It couldn't be missed. The telescopes and binoculars were unnecessary. It could clearly be seen with the naked eye. In fact, it was too bright to view with a telescope or binoculars. The comet tore across the sky, turning night into near-daylight. It had a brilliant nova, with a long, tail that widened like a broom as it came overhead. The broom was opaque, full of comet dust and stuff. Stilmaker was correct in his analogy. It did indeed look like a giant, life-giving sperm. Soon, the broom of the comet widened so much that it covered the sky. Martin Boes didn't like the look of it, didn't like the look of it at all, but said nothing. At home in his back yard, Stilmaker didn't like the look of it at all, either. "What's wrong, Honey?" asked his wife Bambi. "Aren't you excited about your comet?" Stilmaker lowered his binoculars. "It's not *my* comet." He shook his head sadly, as if his worst fears were confirmed. He knew *something bad* was about to happen. "I'm sorry, dear. Maybe I worry too much…" He started to say something else, but changed his mind. He hugged and kissed his wife. They watched the comet pass overhead, then they went back inside and he had pastrami on rye with soup, and they retired for the evening.

As the comet passed overhead, Martin Boes was ready. Soleil was taking photos and videos of the event as Martin Boes reached into his pocket and pulled out a little box. "I have something for you" he said to Soleil. Soleil lowered her camera.

"Oh? What?" He handed her the little box. "What's this?' She opened the box and there was the most exquisite diamond ring she had ever seen. It was a fabulous chunk of ice, set in a platinum mount surrounded by big red rubies, her favorite color. The comet overhead reflected in it, the ring glittering in a dazzling display of lights. She gasped, stricken speechless by its beauty. "Is… is this for me?

"No, I just wanted you to look at it… *of course it's for you!*" Martin Boes knelt gallantly. "Soleil, will you marry me?" Soleil gasped. She looked at him, then at the ring, then back at him. Tears filled her eyes. Nobody noticed his proposal, as they were all looking up at the passing comet.

"Yes, Martin Boes, I will marry you." They kissed and embraced as the comet slowly receded into the East. She tried on the ring. It fit perfectly. "How did you know my ring size?" she sniffed.

"Oh, I have my ways. A little bird told me. His name was Mikey." Soleil was in tears. "You can call me *Honey* now."

"Hmm. Are you sure? I'm still seeing stars from the last time I did that."

"No, no, no, you can call me *Honey*. Go ahead."

"Okay, H— you know what? That's really a very outdated term of affection. I'll call you Soleil."

She looked at him, tears streaming down her beautiful cheeks, tears she had never cried before in her life. "I love you, *Honey*."

"I love you too, Soleil."

# CHAPTER 20

## The Taking of Red

JOSH WOKE UP at 5:30 AM. Tramp, their white German Shepherd, was barking loud, and all the neighborhood dogs were barking, too. Sleepily, Josh went downstairs from his room. From the staircase, he could see Tramp just sitting there and barking. Josh blinked. He rubbed his eyes and blinked again. He heard a high-pitched tone in his ears. *Something was weird.* In the dim light, Tramp seemed to be barking at nothing. "Tramp!" shouted Josh. Tramp stopped barking, then looked at Josh and started barking again, this time with a snarl- it was as if Tramp didn't recognize him. His fur was ruffled and his ears were down. He snapped at Josh when he tried to come near, baring his big white teeth. "Tramp! Tramp! What's wrong? Doncha' know me?" Jody woke up and angrily yelled out of her door. "Josh, will you leave him alone? I'm trying to get some sleep, if you don't mind!"

"I'm not doing nothing! He's acting weird!"

"Probably 'cause *you're* acting weird!' said Jodie. "I swear! I didn't do nothing! He won't *shut up!*" Jodie gave an angry sigh and slammed her door. Tramp kept on barking, louder and with more urgency. Josh heard sirens in the distance."Tramp, shut up!" yelled Josh. But Tramp wouldn't stop barking. Jodie had enough. She got up, flounced out the door, down the stairs to the living room, ready to give it to Josh and Tramp good. On the third step, she saw Josh. Jodie screamed. Josh looked at Jodie. Josh screamed. Tramp barked. The sirens were coming closer. They heard a big crash in the distance. *"What's all the noise?"* yelled Bren, who came downstairs. Bren saw her children. Her children saw her. She screamed. Her children screamed. *"What the hell's going on down there?"* yelled Jimbo, half-asleep. He heard the screams. Jimbo came down the stairs and saw Bren, Josh and Jodie. Bren, Josh and Jodie saw Jimbo. They screamed. Jimbo screamed. Everybody was gray with blue blood veins all over their faces! There was a knock at the door. Jimbo answered it. It was the Garden Gnome. The Garden Gnome screamed.

---

Theresa was in New Orleans, finishing up her wall mural. She was painting one of the series of the "Stylin' Sally" murals that she had been painting for boutiques throughout the South for five years, now. The series depicted a tall stylish fashion model walking down a Café lined Parisian-style street. "Sally" had long blonde hair, big blue eyes and red lips. She wore knee-length shiny red boots- the same boots that Theresa was wearing at the time. Sally appeared to be walking up the street with her head turned back, looking at the viewer. The "Stylin' Sally" series was by now very popular, and Theresa was very thankful and grateful to be making a living as an artist. But it wasn't easy… sometimes she would do a mural, and then the customer would short-change her on the promised fee, or even find an excuse to not pay her at all! She had to travel a lot, had to hustle, had to keep the ball rolling.

Theresa was up on her ladder, putting the finishing touches on Sally's face. All in all, things were going well. She was a very good artist, though she would modestly refer to herself as a

"Copyist". She felt, like all the great artists, they were only copying images and putting them on canvas, or walls in her case. Her father was an excellent artist, and Theresa was a chip off the old block. Theresa proved to be a child prodigy in the second grade. She was on the TV and in the newspapers. She was a natural-born artist from Day One. There was no problem getting her art scholarships and degrees. Now, at 44 years old, she was making a comfortable living, being an artist.

Theresa was up close, dabbing flesh color on Sally's face, when suddenly, Sally's Red lips disappeared and her face turned gray. Theresa blinked. She stared hard at Sally's face. She blinked tightly and opened her eyes wide. She heard a high-pitched noise in her ears. *"What the hell...?"* She moved in very close to the painting. It looked like it had been faded from years in the sun! The colors were flat, washed out, lifeless. Then, Theresa raised her paint brush and noticed her hand. Her hand was gray with blue veins all over it. Dogs were barking nearby.

Theresa jumped, nearly falling off the ladder. She put down her brush and turned over her hand, looking at her palms. She rolled up her sleeve and saw that her whole arm was gray, and spider-webbed with blue veins. Theresa came down the ladder. As she did, she noticed that her shiny Red boots were now shiny gray. And as she got to the ground, she saw that "Stylin' Sally's" shiny red boots were now gray, too. Theresa heard urgent, raised voices nearby. Suddenly, there was the terrible crash of a car collision not far away. A few seconds later, there was another one. Car horns honked and held. People were now yelling. Theresa was very alarmed. She thought she was having a stroke, like her father had. But she felt all right- there was no pain or numbness in her arms or legs. She took three deep breaths. She grabbed her formerly red paint cloth, which now appeared dingy gray. The high-pitched noise got worse. Theresa felt dizzy. She teetered and fell off the ladder. One of her formerly red plastic boots snagged a rung, breaking her fall, but also breaking her ankle with an audible pop. She groaned in pain, hanging upside down. *"Oh God! Oh God! Oh God!"* Suddenly, a big, black dog came into the boutique. It saw Theresa and started barking viciously. In her upside-down view she saw the dog barking deliriously, out of its mind. It barked at Theresa, as if she were treed prey. "DAMN DOG, GET OUTTA HERE! GET!" shouted Theresa. The dog barked even louder, and came towards Theresa. It was frothing at the mouth, growling. "GET BACK! GIT! BAD DOG!". Outside was utter chaos. Everybody was shouting and running around. Sirens were everywhere. She heard another collision. More dogs barked. The high-pitched noise now filled her head. The dog kept coming. Theresa grabbed a rung and managed to pull herself up just as the dog lunged. The dog chomped on Theresa's hair, pulling out tufts in his powerful jaws. Theresa screamed and clambered up the ladder, out of reach from the dog. She unengaged her broken foot and looked down at the dog, which still had her hair in his mouth. The dog tried the first two rungs of the ladder and stood there on two legs, barking up at Theresa "HELP! HELP! HELP ME! IS ANYBODY HERE? HELP!", she screamed at the top of her lungs. Nobody was there. She looked around for anyone. She heard people yelling and running in the distance. She heard yet another car collision. She heard the winding hum of the old Civil Defense siren from 1944 being started up. She thought maybe all the nukes had gone off, but there was no flash, no explosion. Everything was still there, but the colors of things looked strange- flat and lifeless. Theresa remembered her mural. She looked at "Stylin' Sally". Her mural was ruined. It looked as if it had baked in the sun for years. There was no Red color. The dog was still barking, waiting at the foot of the ladder to get her if she should come down. "ANYONE HERE?" she yelled. She looked down at her paint pots. Something was wrong. The paint pot marked "Blue" now held green paint. The paint pot marked "Green" now held blue paint. And the paint pot marked "Red" now held a pale gray *goop*. She stared hard at the gray goop that once was Red. *"Am I losing my mind?"* She blinked. Her ankle throbbed with dull pain. The high-pitched noise abated, but it was still there. Though she didn't know what was happening, she felt relieved that it wasn't just her. *Everybody* was running around acting confused and crazy with chaos outside. She was going to be stuck up at the top of the ladder for a while until somebody came by, so she figured not to panic, and take stock of the situation. She closed her eyes tight and counted to ten. She opened her eyes and looked at the mural. It was hideous, ghastly. "Shit!" she said angrily, throwing the formerly red paint cloth at the barking dog. "Now, I'll *never* get paid!"

---

"We interrupt this program to bring you a special news alert. I'm Roger Dean with Kathy Curtis. We are receiving unconfirmed reports of very strange weather conditions in Los Angeles and outlying areas. Reports of the sky turning green and grass turning blue are streaming in from all over the L.A. basin and, as I've just learned, all over the state. We are told that a green, smoggy haze has filtered into the atmosphere in Yucca Valley and San Bernardino County. Kathy, what do you have on this?"

"Good morning, Dean. Talk about strange weather! We've just gotten numerous reports of, get this- green skies and blue trees and grass from all over California and western states."

Martin Boes blinked. He squeezed his eyes tight shut. And reopened them again. Same thing. He blinked again. Same thing. Something was wrong with the color of things. He was watching news on TV when the new color changes occurred. All of a sudden, there was no red. "Lousy TV!" he muttered. He grabbed the remote and punched up "MENU" and selected "COLOR". He pushed the color scale all the way to the right. There was still no red. "Lousy TV!" he said out loud. He looked all around the room. The colors were the same as on the TV. He turned off the TV set. He heard a high-pitched tone in his ears. He punched himself on the leg. He slapped his face. Same thing. He turned the TV on again. The newscasters all had gray skin with blue-green veins. They were looking at their hands. He looked at his hands. They, too, were gray and were fraught with veins.

He got up, looked in the mirror. His face was now gray and mapped with veins. His first thought was that he was having a stroke or a seizure, or maybe a heart attack. His heart pounded with fear. He took deep breaths and exhaled. He felt OK, except for his heart pounding. No numbness in his arms. He had heard of stroke victims seeing strange colors just before a stroke. He got up, went to the window. He looked out at the panoramic view. The skies were *green*, with fluffy white clouds. Trees and grass were *blue*. There was nothing red, no red anywhere. He noticed down below that there was some kind of disturbance. He heard the ambulances arriving at all the vehicle collisions. He saw gray people getting out of their cars and walking around, looking high and low in confusion. They waved their arms and shouted at one another, as if asking *"What the hell happened?"* Martin Boes settled down now, realizing it wasn't just him. He heard a terrible car collision down below. He thought about Soleil. He grabbed his iPhone 7 and rung up Soleil. There was no answer after ten rings. She was out. He rang up Stilmaker. "Stilmaker."

"This is Martin Boes. What the hell happened?"

"What the hell do you mean by 'what the hell happened', snapped back Stilmaker. In the iPhone 7 screen, Stilmaker's face was gray and covered with veins. It looked like he had two black eyes. Martin Boes went back to the bathroom mirror and glanced at himself. He still had gray skin criss-crossed with blue veins and had double black eyes. "There's something wrong outside. The colors are all *strange*."

"You see it, too? Thank Gah, I thought it was just me! I

thought I was having a stroke! Do you hear a high-pitched tone in your ears?"

"Yes I do!" said Martin Boes, relieved. It wasn't just him. "It… it's everywhere! I looked outside, and people are going berserk. What's going on?"

*"How the hell should I know?"* Stilmaker paused, exhaled. "I think it's a side-effect of the comet coming so close to the earth. Remember what I said about the comet's tail? Maybe… maybe it was caused by the comet. I was afraid something like this would happen. We are still in the comet's tail, you know. My best guess is that something in the comet's tail, like gases or chemicals, has somehow distorted the color spectrum. I didn't think *this* would happen… of course a comet has never come as close to Earth before, except for the one 65 million years ago. Yes, that *must* be the explanation for this. That comet came too close, somehow distorting the wave-lengths of the color spectrum. We are still within range of the comet's tail"

Martin Boes scoffed. "Are… are you sure?"

"Not at all! Like I said, that is my best guess. This never happened before!"

"We need to talk."

"Yes we do. I'll be downtown in one hour. I have to make some calls. Meet me at your Boes-Soleil Café, if it is open."

"Okay. Don't drive, it sounds like a lot of car accidents happening. There are sirens everywhere… traffic's stopped. I'll send Mike to pick you up."

"I hear them, too. Give me two hours. I'll see you there. Good-bye."

"Good-bye." Martin Boes put down the iPhone and watched the TV. The gray newscasters were describing how the sudden color changes were all over the city, then the state, then the country, and finally the world. There was much confusion. The newscasters urged everyone watching not to panic, to remain calm. All regular programming was pre-empted.

Andy and Bill were trimming trees in their brand new, modern cherry picker. It's arm unfolded up to 60 feet in the air, then folded back up and tucked away in the side of the truck. Today, they were trimming evergreen trees in Washington State. Andy was in the cherry picker trimming and Bill was down below in the truck reading the newspaper. Andy pushed the toggle switch up to lop off some branches with his one-handed chainsaw. It was a breeze to lop off big branches with one arm and let them fall. Bill would pick them up when he was done and put the branches in the wood chipper, also included on the truck. Andy smoked a cigarette and buzzed away leisurely. It was a cushy job with big pay and easy hours. They got to work in the outdoor fresh air and beautiful scenery.

Andy toggled left, avoiding the nearby old-fashioned step transformer and the electric wires that were enveloped by the evergreen. It was his job to keep the tree growth off the wires. He toggled up to one of the branches that interfered with the wires. Using his chainsaw, he easily lopped off part of the branch, when two squirrels ran up the branch and bit him on his arm! He batted them away and they came back and attacked him again. He swiped at them with his chainsaw, getting one. It dropped to the street. The other one took off..

*"What the hell?"*

Squirrels never attacked him or anyone like that before. He thought they must have rabies. He toggled back and looked at the squirrel bites, the arm of the cherry-picker coming close to the old transformer. Bill said "What happened?"

"I don't know, these damn squirrels just ran up and bit me." He looked at his arm. The bites were minor, nothing to stop work over. "Are you all right?"

"I guess so. Did a squirrel ever bite you before?"

"Nawp. Hey, are you sure you're all right? They might have rabies, ya know."

"Yah, I'm OK, it's not too bad. *Weird.*" Andy went back to work, and Bill went back to his newspaper. Andy toggled back up, forgetting that he was too close to the transformer. Suddenly, the colors of things changed. Andy heard a loud whining pitch in his ears. The trees were blue. The sky was green. Andy was in a trance, his finger still on the toggle which was going up. He was in a state of confusion. The cherry picker arm was getting closer and closer to the transformer wire. Andy's lit cigarette dropped from his frozen lips into his shirt pocket. The cherry picker arm was pressing up on the transformer wire. The hydraulic arm whirred. Bill noticed that something was not right. He put down the newspaper and looked out the cab just in time to see the hydraulic arm snap the wire off the step transformer. "ANDY!" shouted Bill. The transformer exploded, and the live wire whipped off, falling into the cherry picker, giving Andy a dose of fifty thousand volts of electricity. Andy was still standing frozen with his finger on the toggle switch. Down below, Bill also got zapped with fifty thousand volts. He was dead. So was Andy, though he remained frozen in standing position, his finger still stuck on the toggle switch. Up, up, up in the air went Andy. The hydraulic arm unfolded and reached up to its full length, sixty feet in the air. The lit cigarette in Andy's pocket ignited his clothing, and combined with the electrical high voltage, turned Andy into a flaming, burning beacon high in the emerald green sky.

---

Something was definitely not right at the Huntington Library and Botanical Gardens in San Marino, California. There was a museum security alert. Something had happened to Pinkie and Blue Boy! Security rushed to the room where the famous duet was installed. A crowd of people gathered around the protective barricade, gawking and gasping at Pinkie and Blue Boy. The paintings appeared faded, dull as if defaced by someone throwing acid on them. They were ghastly. The people looking at them didn't look so good, either. Thomas

Gainsborough's *Blue Boy,* painted in 1770, was now *Green Boy.* The famous blue satin costume worn by the subject now appeared *green.* Blue boys face was a pasty, blotchy, washed out gray. There was no hint of flesh tone to be seen.

*Pinkie,* which was painted a quarter century later in 1794 by Thomas Lawrence, had completely lost her pinkness. She looked like a faded ghost. Her pink hat with the long trailing ribbon and her pink bodice were a blotchy gray, as was her face. There was utter confusion in the gallery, with expressions like:

"What the?"

"Do you see what *I* see?"

"Do you hear a noise?"

"What's happening?"

"*Oh my God*!" "Look!"

"What is going on?"

"Look at your hands!"

"Oh, my Lord!"

"Good God!"

"Call 911!"

"Okay, I'm calling…" A man got his cell phone and pushed 911. " Uh…What do I tell 'em?" It didn't matter, because 911 was already swamped with emergency calls, and would be for several days.

Outside in the Japanese Gardens, there was more chaos. The famous Red arched bridge that spanned the garden scream now appeared a pale, washed out gray. The award winning cultured Red roses were now gray, as was any previous Red flower in the garden. The sky was *green.* The trees and grass appeared *blue.* A man had a heart attack and died, falling flat on his back onto the lush blue grass. People were running around screaming in shock at each other's ugliness. Security could only stand there, dumfounded. They were ugly, too.

Near Jubilee Gardens, The Passengers on the London Eye Ferris wheel were treated to a rather unusual panoramic view. Something other than else!

At 135 meters, The London Eye was the world's tallest cantilevered wheel, with 40 kilometer panoramic views on a clear day. The gradual flight in one of the 32 high-tech glass capsules took approximately 30 minutes. Night or day, The London Eye offered spectacular views of London and its famous landmarks such as Big Ben, Buckingham Palace, St Paul's Cathedral, Westminster Abbey and Trafalgar Square. This day was different. There were forty-five people in just one of the spacious glass capsules on the wheel. When the wheel hit the top this time, they were still treated with the spectacular view of London and the Thames, but something was wrong with the color of things. The sky was Emerald Green, as far as the eye could see. The giant maze in Trafalgar Square, and all the grass and trees around it were blue. The Thames was still there, it was a beautiful aquamarine. Jubilee Gardens was blue. And there was no red to be seen. The famous London Red double-decker buses, which could be seen everywhere, were now gray! They carried ghastly crews of sickly gray passengers.

The panorama view was still there, but it seemed flat, faded. It looked like a grandiose mural that had faded in the sun. There was no depth. It was as though a giant painted canvas had been wrapped around the high tech glass capsule, and you were being asked to believe it was real. All the passengers in all the high-tech glass capsules were stunned, especially when they turned and noticed each other. They all heard high-pitched squeals in their heads. Some believed they were having heart attacks and seizures. Some were so convinced they were having a heart attack, they actually brought on a heart attack, because they believed so. Some died. Some suffered seizures. Some fainted from shock. All passengers were evacuated, and the London Eye was shut down for the time being, until they could figure out what happened.

He was tired of running. He was tired of hiding. He thought he should have been dead and in the arms of Allah, long ago. He was tired of living in fear. He was tired of living in caves. He was tired of goats. He was tired of being Number One on the Ten Most Wanted Terrorist list. He was tired of being the worst villain since Hitler. And so, several years before the comet event, he faked his own death.

He made a deal with corrupt Pakistani officials and substituted his exact look alike double into the firefight, where he was killed by the Navy Seals. He was reported dead. The media went wild. Seizing the opportunity, the President of the United States interrupted national television late at night to report to the American people that he had been killed. Wild cheer and celebration ensued! His death was an event, a happening, a holiday! Tears of joy were wept upon hearing of the death of this man who had done so much wrong. Osama Bin Laden was dead! Only minutes after the President's message was delivered, it was discovered that that the body was *not* that of Osama.

*Yikes.*

But the Media circus had begun. Everybody was celebrating. The 9/11 victim's families were spotlighted. The President had spoken, scoring big points and making tremendous political hay. But the body was *not* Osama.

*What to do, what to do?*

They couldn't just say *"Oops, sorry, our mistake, it wasn't him"* or *"Never mind! We got the wrong guy. Our mission has failed."* Nobody wanted to hear that, now. Not now, after the big celebration of National Pride! So the Powers That Be hushed it up. They buried the body at sea at once so the body was gone, and beyond DNA testing. They used DNA supplied by the corrupt Pakistani officials to prove his "death". And Osama was relocated to a mountain cave by the Pakistani government's Reformed Former Terrorist Protection Program, where he lived in his lush, customized cave. He became just another anonymous cave dweller, except that he was rich. He had to pay off his corrupt officials every month, but that was not a problem. The money was there. But, no more terrorism! That was part of the deal. There would be no more *Jihads*, no more killing the *Western Devils,* no more blowing things up, and no more mass murder! None of that stuff.

Osama settled into his new lodgings easily. The weight of the world was off his shoulders. He was no longer hunted like a dog. He could finally relax and enjoy the few good years he had left. Osama was deep inside his underground cave. He had all the luxuries of a rich man, all the best electronics and computers. His cave suite was floored with exquisite parquetry and the finest rugs from Afghanistan. He had all the best movies, games and Internet. He watched football. He would anonymously play interactive modern warfare games with people all over the world on his big HD flat screen. Teenagers in Wenatchee, Washington had no idea that they were playing video games with Osama Bin Laden. His self-contained power supply and connections could not be traced. He had all the best creature comforts, so he did not have to emerge from his cave very often. When he did, he had the best security people escort him in safety. He had to stay hidden at all times. There were many who would love to rat him out.

Osama was reading an *Asterix & Obelix* comic book, when there was a knock on his door."Who is it?" asked Osama, alerted, because they usually called him before knocking. "It is I, Fazed!" Fazed was Osama's most trusted guard. Osama peered out the peep-hole of the door. "Just a second!" He had to unlock all the locks, taking a couple of minutes. Finally, he opened the door. Fazed rushed in and slammed the door behind him, relocking all the locks. "What is it? What's wrong?' asked Osama. Fazed turned and looked at him, up and down. Then, he looked all around at the cave suite. "Osama! Dou you not see?" he said, eyes wide open, blinking. "Shhhh!

Don't call me that! It's *"sir"*. I see fine, you idiot! What are you talking about?"

"Sir! Look at yourself! Look at your hands!' Osama smiled and blinked and looked at his hands, humoring Fazed. "Yes? They are my hands, what about them?"

"Can you not see? Look at your face, sir, your face!" Shaking his head, Osama went to the full-length mirror and looked at his face. His image reflected the same well-known and despised Osama Bin Laden as always, but with grayer hair. Fazed rushed up beside him in the mirror. He gazed at his face. "See, sir? See the veins? He looked at Osama's face and then back in the mirror. "What the hell's wrong with you, Fazed? What am I supposed to be seeing?—*veins?*"

"Look at me, sir! Look at me! Do I look different to you?" Osama looked hard at Fazed, not appreciating the tone of familiarity Fazed used. Clearly, he was upset about something. "No… you're still my favorite bodyguard— you've put on a little weight, maybe. Why are you so hot and sweaty? Go wash up, now!"

"But, sir! Outside! Outside there is something strange happening! The colors! Outside! The colors have changed! The people are yellow! Blood is yellow! The sky is green! The trees are blue! You must see! Outside…"

"Are you out of your mind? Quit your babbling nonsense and calm down! The *colors*, you say? I see nothing wrong with the colors! Are you high on hashish again? I told you not to do that! If you were not my favorite bodyguard, I would…"

"You must come up, sir! You must come up! You must see for yourself!"

"I will not! I will not emerge like a marmot directly into a trap! Not until you explain what's going on!"

"It is as I said, sir! Something happened to the color outside! It has… changed. I cannot explain it" you will have to see for yourself!"

"I see—what do you mean when you say, 'blood is yellow?"

"Yes, sir! Blood is yellow!" Osama pulled out a knife and pricked his thumb. He saw the red drop of blood come out. He held his thumb out to Fazed. "Does my blood look yellow to you?"

"Yes, Osama!"

"Will you quit calling me that? Ah, now I see!" said Osama, nodding knowingly. "You are color-blind, my friend. But don't worry, it is not a thing that will affect your job performance."

"But, Os—sir!" bleated Fazed "Others outside see the same things I do! It is not just me!" Osama was concerned now. His blood was red, and he saw no problems in his cave suite. Perhaps there was a gas attack up above. He didn't want to risk capture, after all these years. Of course, he had the same thoughts every time he did emerge. This was something new. "Is... *is it safe*? Is it safe to come outside? I thought I heard an explosion."

"Yes, sir! I will guard you with my life, as always! Stay behind me, if you please. It is chaos outside!" Osama stared hard at Fazed's face, trying to detect any falseness in his eyes. Fazed seemed genuinely truthful.

"You'd better be right about this. Remember what happened to my look-alike. I can arrange something similar for you, if you are entertaining any thoughts of betraying me."

"I swear to Allah, sir!

"Okay, I'll come up. But this had better not be some kind of joke for my amusement!"

"I swear to Allah!" Osama put on a personal gas mask, just in case. He re-arranged his burka to cover the mask and his all-too-familiar beard. As he followed Fazed to the entrance to the cave, he had misgivings about emerging. Maybe Fazed was paid off to set him up. He fingered his sharp knife in his pocket, ready to use it on Fazed if he was being ratted out. But

Fazed really seemed terrified, frightened. As Fazed reached the door ahead of him, Osama dropped back into a cul-de-sac and watched. Fazed unlocked the many locks and opened the door. Osama watched as Fazed looked outside, where there was much commotion. Fazed looked around and slowly shook his head. He turned back to Osama "It is still the same as I said, sir!" Osama was enraged. This was nonsense! Colors didn't just change. He was sure Fazed was high on drugs or maybe drunk. He took the last few steps up to the doorway and looked out.

It was just as Fazed had said. The sky was green. The trees were blue. The earth was gray. People were running around with their burkas covering their faces, screaming "Allah! Allah!" Dogs chased goats and people. Goats chased people, ramming them with their heads. Cows ran away. There was an injured man lying on the street with a gaping wound in his gray leg. He was in shock. Instead of red blood, there was opaque yellow blood gushing from his wound! The yellow blood oozed onto the street. Osama looked at Fazed. His face was now gray and covered with veins. Osama looked at his hands. They were gray and covered with veins. He was dumbfounded. He heard a high-pitched noise in his head. He bent down and picked up a blue leaf, holding it up close to his eyes. His eyes filled with confusion. He slowly shook his head. *"What have the Western Devils done, now?"* he said to no one in particular.

Fearful, Osama fled back to his underground cave suite, expecting everything to be all right down there. But it was not all right. Blue was green and green was blue down there, too. And there was no Red. His plush carpets of red, purple and violet were now faded and washed out. The drop of blood still on his finger was now yellow. Osama took off his gas mask, lowered his burka and looked in the mirror. His face was gray with veins spider-webbing all over it. He looked like he had two black eyes. He looked dreadful, ghoulish, like walking death. Osama blinked. He heard a high-pitched noise in his ears. He *knew* he shouldn't have come up! *"Allah! What have I done to deserve this?"* wailed Osama.

---

There was trouble at the local supermarket. People were stumbling around the aisles, looking all around, crashing their carts into each other's. They couldn't believe their eyes. In the meat department, customers complained about rotten steaks being sold as fresh. Upon investigation, the butcher found that the steaks and all other red meat products, stacked in neat rows in their bins, were all rotten looking. They were all a sickly gray. The chuck roasts, ground round, beef ribs, cube steaks, *filet mignons*, London Broils, livers, T-bones, the veal; all the red meats were all gray. The lamb chops wrapped in their pink paper diapers paper was gray in gray paper. The pork chops, ground pork and pork sausages were all dingy yellow. They looked spoiled. The packaged chicken breasts, legs, wings and thighs were gray. There was no pink to be seen. It was the same with the turkey. A little farther down the aisle, the butcher found gray lobsters, gray crabs and gray shrimp. Red Snapper was now Gray Snapper.

Over in the produce section, things were even wackier! The celery was blue. Avocados were cobalt blue. Cucumbers were dark blue. Broccoli was blue. Zucchini was blue. String beans were blue. Bell peppers were blue. Green onions were blue. Watermelons were blue on the outside, yellow on the inside. Cabbages were blue. So was lettuce. Spinach was blue. Collard greens were blue. Brussels sprouts were blue. Anything green was now blue.

Potatoes were yellow. Onions were yellow. Mushrooms were gray. Radishes were gray. Garlic was yellow. Baby Red potatoes were gray. Red onions were gray. Squash was blue or yellow. Eggplant was almost blue. Tomatoes were gray. Carrots were gray. Parsnips were yellow and blue. Red cabbage was dark gray. Red bell peppers were gray. Apples that were previously red were now gray. Apples that were previously green were now blue. Yellow apples stayed yellow. Oranges were gray. Plums were gray-green. Limes were blue. Lemons remained yellow. Red grapes were gray. Green grapes were blue. Purple grapes were gray-teal. Cumquats were yellow. Persimmons were gray. Peaches were gray. Unripe pears were blue. Strawberries, cherries, raspberries and cranberries were now all gray. Blueberries were green. Papayas were blue. Mangos were gray. Blackberries, blueberries, Boysenberries, Loganberries and Huckleberries- if any- were shades of dark green and gray.

In their shopping carts, people noticed that their multi-packs of Coca-Cola were now gray! They could still see the logo with the familiar white flowing script and the undulating swash. Their cans of Campbell soup were now gray, recalling the "Pop-Art" prints of the sixties by Andy Warhol. A man in a cowboy hat held up a pack of Marlboros, and wondered when they changed the red pack to gray.

In the deli section, a man was following a nice-looking girl in tight blue denim jeans. The jeans fit her lithe, supple body perfectly. The man wanted to get acquainted with her. He followed behind her for a minute, and then noticed that her blue denim jeans were green! He thought it was odd, though he had seen denim in other colors before. He pushed his cart beside hers. "Do you come here often?" The girl turned and looked at him, studying his face. He saw her face. It was an ugly pale gray, criss-crossed with green veins! It looked like she had two black eyes. He heard a high-pitched noise in his head. "Umm… never mind, I was just kidding, have a great day!" He moved on with his cart. He noticed that she kept staring at him. As he walked away, he looked back and saw the girl put her hand over her mouth, her eyes wide open. He wondered if his fly was open. He looked down. The barn door was closed. He shrugged and moved on. It was only when he saw his reflection in the freezer case that he understood why she stared at him like that. The people in the store were all outraged at the rotten food being sold, but when they took a gander at themselves and each other, they quickly shut up. *They* looked pretty rotten, too. Everybody looked rotten.

---

The tagger was making the finishing touches on his mural when something went wrong. He looked out at the cement canyon that was the Los Angeles River. It was beautiful, in its way. There were some scenic vistas here and there with sections that were remnants of the river before it was paved over. There were marsh sections with cat-tails. There was wildlife with visiting birds like cranes and egrets. There were ducks, pigeons, crows, foxes and even coyotes. The coyotes still roamed the river up and down as they had for centuries. Any tagger worth his salt had murals here. Some were quite talented and produced graffiti that was worthy of the walls of Rome. Here was an ideal place to work, virtually unhindered. The taggers could see the police and Harbor Patrol coming a mile away.

The tagger shrugged and went back to work on his mural. The bold, giant, multicolored letters with red shadows and outlines shouted out his representation. The tagger grabbed the can of red spray can and dropped the cap on the ground. He shook the can and made a long red outline around his signature. When his outline was joined the red turned gray. The tagger blinked. He shook the can again and sprayed. Gray paint came out instead of red. The tagger knelt down and looked very closely at the paint. *Como esta?*

He shook the can, weighed it. It still had plenty inside. He sprayed a spot again. The red was still gray. He looked down at the red spray can cap before him. It was now gray. The tagger stopped. It was then that he noticed that all the red color on his mural was gone. The green paint was blue. The blue paint was green. His mural looked flat, shallow, and *lifeless*. There was no depth. The tagger looked around, still kneeling. The sky was green. The tagger wondered if the spray paint fumes were affecting him. Then he noticed his arms and hands. They were gray, with olive-green veins. He jumped, falling on his back. He looked at his legs. They were pale gray and covered with veins. The tagger was stunned. His mural was ruined. He heard a bad car crash nearby. Someone was yelling over a loudspeaker. The Sheriff's helicopter zoomed overhead in the green sky. The tagger was not concerned about being caught right now, he had other problems. The helicopter zoomed by, not concerned with catching taggers at this moment. They had their own issues to attend to. The tagger heard sirens all around. He expected the cops to be there any second. But the cops never came. He heard another car crash. Then, the Harbor Patrol truck raced by the concrete river at full speed, with flashing *white* lights instead of *Red*. They completely ignored the tagger. The tagger wondered why they didn't stop. He dropped the spray can. He lay on his back looking up at the green sky, totally defeated.

---

It was a symbol of everything the Stone Age could achieve. In Southern England, on the Salisbury Plain, Stonehenge stood, as it had for five thousand years. The sarcens, bluestones, pylons, menhirs, monoliths, digits and slabs were dragged to this spot from quarries miles away and placed on this spot in a circular temple formation. There they stayed.

Some say it was a calendar. Some say it was a sacrificial temple. Some say it was an early wrist-watch. Some say it was an alien landing site. Some say it was a message to the gods. Some say it was a maze. Some say it was an early observatory. Some say it tracked comets…

Some say Pagans made it. Some say Druids made it. Some say Pagan Druids made it. Some say Neanderthals made it. Some say the aliens made it. Some say the Scots made it. Some say the Welsh made it. Some say the Irish made it. Some say the English made it. Some say the Andorrans made it. Some say the Spanish made it. Some say the Goths made it. Some say Uther Pendragon made it. Some say the first astronomer made it.

No matter what it was, or who made it, the rust-colored lichen covered monument (or what was left of it) still stood, as if in mute laughter at all those who could not figure out who it was made by and for what purpose. Its purpose now was as a world-famous tourist attraction. At the moment, it was closed to the public for the day. The nearby parking lot was empty, except for security. Stonehenge stood alone once again on the green Salisbury Plain. Then in just a few moments, the Salisbury Plain turned blue! The skies above Stonehenge turned green! Any rust-colored lichens on the monument were now pale yellow. Any green lichens turned blue-gray. The bluestones were now greenstones. There were no warm colors on Stonehenge, now. The lone security guard came outside his post and saw the new Stonehenge and the new, blue Salisbury Plain. He raced back into the office and alerted the authorities.

The color changes were not so hard on Stonehenge. It was just a bunch of old rocks. But if Stonehenge *could* have said something… if it *could* create an abstract thought… if it *could* register some kind of emotion in its stony brain and express it outwardly, it would probably be something along the lines of: "WHAAAAAAA?"

---

"Mus' Richard! "Mus' Richard!" There was a loud banging on the door of Martin Boes' son Rickey's room in the Malibu Beach house. "Mus' Richard! Mus' Richard!" It was 6AM and the dawn's early light was just unfurling outside. Rickey was sound asleep after one of his wild nights out. Rickey looked at the clock. His room was still dark. "Mus Richard! Mus' Richard!" There was more banging. It was old Farnsworthy.

This was unusual to Rickey, because Farnsworthy *never* got excited, *never* banged on doors. Something must be wrong. Rickey wrapped the blanket around his naked body and stumbled to the door. He unlocked it and opened the door. There was Farnsworthy in his pajamas, trembling, although it wasn't very cold. His face was rather pale. "Farns? What is it?" said Rickey, still half asleep. "Oh, Mus' Richard! A terrible thing has happened! Me eyes ha'gone bad… I'm afraid I mun' resign from your service… 'tes terrible… I canna see straight, and what I do see is all amok!"

"What's wrong, Farns? What do you see?" asked Rickey, patiently. Rickey knew Farnsworthy was 96 years old, so it was no surprise that something might go wrong with the old guy at any time. This might be the time. "Are you all right, Farns? Do you feel Okay?"

"Yes, Mus' Richard, I feel fine…'tes strange, I don't look fine, nor does anything else. The sky is green, the grass is blue… things are all switched around… I canna see red… aye,'tes terrible… me time has come!" "Easy there, Farns, easy! You're probably just going color blind, you'll be all right… gimme a sec, and I'll take you down to the clinic in a bit—you probably just need some glasses."

"I dunna' think so, Mus' Richard… don't 'ee see it, too?" Rickey went back into the still dark room, put on his boxers and grabbed his blue denim jeans. "See what, Farns?" Farnsworthy went to the big window and pressed a button, activating the solar-powered motorized window shades. The shades slowly, smoothly opened up, letting light into the room. When the curtains were opened, the view of Malibu was completely different. Rickey saw the *green* sky. The ocean was a *teal* color. The trees and bushes were *blue*. Rickey stood there, puzzled. "What the hell…?" he muttered. Then he looked at the denim blue jeans in his hand. They were *green!* Then he looked at his hand and arm. It was pale gray, and crises-crossed with green veins. He heard the high-pitched tone in his head. *"What is this...?"*

"Do 'ee see it, Mus' Richard? Do 'ee see it? Can ye hear it?"

"I see it. I hear it, too." Rickey Boes looked at Farnsworthy. He looked like a rotting corpse. Rickey screamed. Farnsworthy screamed when he saw Rickey. "Oh my God!" said Rickey, staring out the window in disbelief at the new colors. "They musta shot off the nukes!"

"Aye, tes terrible! Mus' Richard!" Farnsworthy broke down in tears and ran to Rickey, embracing him. Rickey held the sobbing Farnsworthy in his arms, as though in a Madonna and Child portrait.

They both just stared out the window, wondering what to do next.

---

Soleil woke up at seven as usual. She went into the bathroom and sat down on the toilet. The lights were still low. She flushed, and went to the sink to wash her hands. She turned on the light fixtures above the sink and looked in the mirror. Soleil blinked. Her beautiful formerly brown eyes widened as never before in her life.

The beauteous Soleil looked like a zombie at a Halloween party. Her face was pale gray, with no flesh color to be seen. Her face was mapped with green blood veins all over. Her eyes appeared as if she had suffered two black eyes in a fight. Her large breasts were spider-webbed with repulsive veins. So were her legs and backside. Her silken chestnut hair was now an ugly dishwater grayish yellow. Her neck was sickly gray with the major arteries most apparent. She blinked her eyes tight for ten seconds and looked again. The view was the same. Soleil took off all her clothes and went to the full-length mirror. Her entire body was pale gray and translucent. She could faintly see the colors of her intestines and organs. There were veins crises-crossing her entire body, every inch of it. She turned around and looked at her back side. It was the same there, too. Soleil screamed. She sank to the floor, stunned. Was she sick? She didn't feel sick. She heard a high-pitched tone in her ears. It wouldn't stop. *What happened?*

She didn't use drugs or drink excessively. She had 20-20 vision. She was in shock. She thought about Martin Boes. She looked at her diamond and ruby engagement ring. The rubies were gray, ugly. She jumped up and ran to get her iPhone7. She rang up Martin Boes, switching off the video call option this time. She wasn't going to let Martin Boes, or anyone else see her like *this*. His number rang, but there was no answer, after twelve rings. She switched on the Internet. She noticed something weird about the screen of her phone. It seemed flat, drab, missing of something, but she wasn't sure what. She cycled her phone, basically rebooting it because it was more of a computer that a phone. She got the same results. *"What is wrong?"* she said to herself. Suddenly, she saw a pattern, realized that a certain color was missing from the displays. That color was *red*.

---

The three stoners had just scored some *Train Wreck* marijuana from the local dispensary in Oakland, California. *Oaksterdam*, as it was commonly called was the unofficial capital of marijuana in the United States. Marijuana was now legal in California and most states, and it was plentiful and cheap. The medical marijuana was the best, since it was grown by the most learned marijuana growers anywhere. Marijuana was now cheap and legal, but if you were caught driving under the influence of it, you were subject to the same punishments as if driving under the influence of alcohol.

The three stoners, Joey, Adam and Roy, unwrapped their new fresh stash of chronic. The smell was just the best. It looked like something off the pages of *High Times* magazine.

"You got the blunt wrap?" said Joey. "Got it", said Adam, producing a wine-flavored brown cigar wrap. They crumbled the sticky *Train Wreck* into a little pile of tobacco and mixed it in well. They rolled a big blunt about nine inches long. They sat down and put on a DVD in 3D Ultra-Def. They all sat down and lit up the big blunt. They inhaled deeply, coughing after trying to hold the smoke in. It was just too strong. Nevertheless, they passed it among each other, the room filling up with the familiar sound of coughing stoners. They cracked up laughing at the movie, which was also about some stoners and their exploits. The smell of skunk filled the room. About halfway through the blunt, Adam said, "Hey... this shit is amazing... *I've never seen these colors before...*"

"Neither have I" said Joey. This shit is incredible!"

"Wow... you guys ain't kidding!" said Roy. I remember back in '11, I had some *Ice Cap* that would change all the colors around, but *nothing* like this! I was at my high school and we were just getting out of English, when we..." He paused, mouth slack, jaws agape, in classic stoner style. "Uh, Roy? Please don't start a long story while holding the blunt!"

"Oh, shit!" said Roy, coughing. "Sorry!" He passed the blunt to Adam. Adam took a courageous hit and passed it to Joey. "This is killer shit, man! Like, the sky in the movie looks green, and the trees and grass look blue! And everybody looks *weird-colored.*"

"Hey you're right! No shit! The sky does look green! And, look! The front lawn of that house is blue! This is some wacky-tobacky!"

"What's that noise? You hear a noise?"

"Yeah it's like a high-pitched tone! Awesome, dude!"

"I hear it too! Hey!"

"Oh yeah, I hear it, too!" yelled Joey. "Check it out!" They all puffed on the blunt and were absorbed in the movie. "Wow, look at that chick! Why is she so gray and ugly? Is she a zombie? Is she going to a costume party?"

"I don't know, I'm too stoned." said Adam.

"Damn! This weed is the *best shit ever!* We'll definitely get some more tomorrow!"

"It's. like acid! I think I'm hallucinating" said Roy.

*"The colors! The colors! Look at the colors"* said Joey.

---

Ron had it. He'd had enough. He was sick of it all, tired of it all, bored by it all, depressed and saddened by it all. Everything was just shit. His life was drab, unexciting. *Bleak*. That's what it was, a Bleak World. There was no passion in his life. He didn't have a wife or a girlfriend. He was real fat. He had no support group to support him. He had no social networking 'page' on the computer, where he could whine and bitch about his lousy life… even if he did, all he would get was comments like "so sorry" or "I feel for you, bro" from strangers who were termed "friends". More likely, he would receive a comment like "Please don't play out your personal drama on this social networking page" or "Quit whining and be happy for what you have." Ron was going to kill himself. He was *really gonna do it!*

Ron hated getting up in the morning. He hated going to work and he hated the people at work who hated him even more. They treated him like a retarded moron. New 'managers' would appear every three months, and he would have to appease these new managers, who didn't know him. The managerial 'clique' focused on somehow getting rid of Ron, because he was fat and old. Ron was so miserable at his job, that he wished that they *would* get rid of him, fire him for incompetency. That way, at least he would get unemployment compensation. But the managers wanted to make him so miserable he would quit, thus receiving no unemployment compensation. This was a common situation in many work places. But it wasn't just the job, for Ron. Sure, he was sick of the rat-race, but so was everybody. Sure, he felt that his life was just a *treadmill to oblivion*, but so did everybody else. All he did was work, come home, eat and sleep, work, come home, eat and sleep. He was paying eight hundred dollars a month for his cracker box one-bedroom apartment with noisy neighbors blasting their stereos. *"What have I got for a thousand a month? A place to shit, shave and shower!"* he thought to himself. Tears welled in his eyes as he felt sorry for himself. He was very lonely, but he wanted it that way. Guys were idiot jerks. He couldn't talk to them. Everything was just a pissing contest, to other guys. Girls wouldn't even *look* at him, much less talk to him; talking to him would have been considered as granting a favor. The fat and ugly girls didn't want him, either. They sure didn't want somebody who reminded them of themselves. He was lonely, but he wouldn't set himself up for rejection. Never again.

So, Ron was going to *do it*, kill himself. Now. He had thought about it for a while. He thought if he was going to *do* it, make sure he *did* it. No fake suicidal "cries for help". If he didn't succeed, they'd lock him up in the mental ward. No thanks. He didn't want to use a gun- what if it turned out non-fatal, and he was a *vegetable*, having to be nursed 24-7? No, thank you. He thought about jumping off the pier, but again, was reminded of the *vegetable* factor. *"If you're gonna do it, make sure ya do it!"* he thought to himself. He thought he'd heard that line in a movie.

Ron decided to slash his wrists in the bath-tub. No muss, no fuss. When they found him, all they'd have to do is pull the plug. He took his clothes off. He drew a nice hot bath. He turned the radio up loud. He got a fresh bottle of whiskey, some brandy, and a forty-ounce beer. He rolled three fatty joints of *Train Wreck,* put the joints in the ashtray, and set the ashtray on the side of the tub. He got his Zippo lighter. He thought again, and put on his underwear so he wouldn't be found totally naked. He didn't want to upset anybody any more than he had to. He put out the box with his ID and most important papers. He was glad he didn't have a dog or cat to worry about. He thought about leaving the obligatory suicide note, and there was much he could have said. But, he didn't want to get into a suicide note, because it might give him second thoughts about what he was trying to do, so he did not write one. He had made his decision. He didn't care how they interpreted his suicide." *Let 'em say whatever the hell they want.*" He went to the tool drawer and got out a single-edge. He took the little cardboard cover off the blade edge. He got in the tub. The water was just right. He sat up in the tub, fired up a joint and opened the whiskey. He drank straight from the bottle. The radio coincidentally played his favorite songs. "*Yes!!!*" he shouted. He took the razor blade. Holding up his arm, he cut three lateral slits into the wrist. He had heard that this was the most certain way to bleed to death. He did the same with the other wrist. The blood gushed out of the slits of his arm, dripping into the bath water. The blood gave the bath water a red wine color. "*Aaccch!*" said Ron, turning away from the unpleasantness and grabbing the whiskey bottle. He drank and drank, chasing the booze down with the beer. He took the biggest hits in his life on the joint, and reveled in his music. He was going to drink himself unconscious, so he wouldn't notice death. With his toes, he turned on the hot water a little more, took another hit, and guzzled some whiskey. After a while, he began to see double. He laughed out loud, it seemed so funny. That was the last thing he remembered before he blacked out.

Ron woke up two hours later. He blinked. His eyes popped open wide. He was still in the tub. The tub was filled with *yellow water*. He jumped up in shock. His arms hurt. He looked at his arms. Yellow blood was oozing, seeping out of his wrists. He remembered then that he had tried to kill himself by slashing his wrists. "*Oh God, what did I do?*" he whispered hoarsely to himself. He heard a high-pitched tone in his head. The tub looked like it was filled with urine. Something clicked in Ron's head when he saw the yellow blood in the tub and coming out his wrists.

Ron wanted to live now, and changed his mind about killing himself. But the damage was done. He tried to get up, but he was extremely drunk and weak from loss of blood. He was very cold. With all his strength, he managed to lurch his body over the side of the tub and plop onto the bathroom floor, creamy yellow blood still oozing from his arms. He took three deep breath sand managed to sit up. He grabbed a towel and tried to wrap it around his wrist, but was unable to do so. He could've called 911, but that would be an invitation to the psycho ward. No thanks. He breathed hard. When he did, the yellow blood gushed out even more. He propped himself up and managed to stand up. Everything seemed green, even the air. He tried to take a step, but his feet were so numb he couldn't feel them. Watching his feet, he took tentative steps on his feet which felt like stumps belonging to someone else. The yellow blood was everywhere. He slipped on his blood, and fell to the linoleum like a whale being dumped on the deck of a Japanese whaler. He breathed deep and got up again. He could feel his feet, but it was pins and needles. He was now an animal in survival mode. He never doubted for a second that he would make it to the kitchen. He fell again, hard, onto the kitchen floor. He moaned in pain.

*"Oh God oh God oh God, why did I do it?"* He cried like a baby. He sat up, snuffled, looked at his arms, remembered that he cut his wrists. He looked up from the floor at the cabinet. *"May be something in there!"* he thought, craftily. Grabbing the drawer pulls and the side of the sink, he pulled himself up to standing position. He opened up the cabinet door. He grabbed the packaging tape gun out and looked at it. He kept forgetting what he was doing. He picked up things and put them down. The radio was now playing *"Red, Red Wine"* by UB40. Ron laughed at the irony of it, forgot that he was bleeding to death again. He remembered again." *Oh, Jesus!"*

He was laughing. His peripheral vision was fading. He could see stars and little birdies traipsing across his vision. *"Uh-oh, tunnel vision! Better get goin'!"* He became mock-serious, as if it were all a joke. He was fading fast, now. Blinking, he saw a roll of silver duct tape. *"That'll do it…",* he said, and grabbing the tape, he used his teeth to tear off a length of duct tape and wrap it around his wrist. This was great energy expenditure, and he could not stand up anymore. *"Think I better sit down"*, he said, judgmentally. He sat down on the kitchen floor, covered in yellow blood. With his last remaining strength, he tore off a piece of duct tape with his teeth, wrapping the duct tape around his other wrist, stopping the blood flow. He thought it was too late. His vision was going from gray to brown, and then black. He remembered something about elevating his legs. He sat back on his big bloody butt, and the last thing he recalled was propping his bloody legs up on the refrigerator, and that song's refrain on the radio…

*"…Red, red, wine make me feel so fine… red, red wine make me feel so fine…*

Myra let the dog back in before she went out in the cold, cold snow. In the year of The Comet, Spokane, Washington had one of the worst snowfalls in its history. There was more than one hundred inches of snow, from Thanksgiving on, until April of the following year. It was January 13th, today. The snow was packed. Everything was blanketed in 3 to 4 feet of snow. The snow-plows were inundated with work, and there were not enough snow plows to go around. If you owned a snow plow, you were indeed one of the lucky ones. Everybody loved you, adored you, and blessed you with money, sex or drugs, if you only scooped out their driveway.

You could not even see the pavement on the smaller roads. The road was covered in 1-2 feet of crushed ice, packed down even harder by the cars and buses, both requiring chains to negotiate roads that would have a cross-country skier grinning with delight. It was something out of *Dr. Zhivago*. Everything was a White Winter Wonderland. All the houses and buildings roofs were blanketed with snow, turning the most squalid hovels into storybook Ice Palaces trimmed with icicles. The icicles could be dangerous: if a big one dislodged from the eaves above, a person could be impaled.

Myra put on some lip balm. She checked her mirror. She was seventy-six years old, but she looked a lot younger, especially from a distance. She had kept up her girlish physique. She was petite and slim. She usually would drive down to the library to check her e-mail and shop for books on the Internet, but the snow was so dangerous, she thought she would take the bus today. She made sure there were some coins in her red plastic coin holder. She put on her red knitted mitts and wrapped her red knitted shawl around her head, so only a small portion of her face was exposed. She buttoned up her overcoat and went out to the bus stop near her house.

There was four feet of snow piled up at the bus stop. The bus bench was covered in snow. Except for the bus stop sign, there was no real indication where the bus stop was. The bus bench was long blanketed over with snow. There was no place to sit or stand, except out in the road. Myra stood about 25 feet away from where the bus stop was. She hoped the bus wouldn't take too long to get there, and hoped the driver would see her when it did. Luckily, after just a few minutes the bus lurched into view. Myra could hear the bus crunching its way on the ice-encrusted road. There was so much snow, it was hard to tell where the local landmarks were. The bus smurshed its way forward, but Myra had to rush out into the street to make sure the driver saw her. The friendly black veteran bus driver slowed down and opened the door. *"Young lady, what are you doing out here in the snow like this?"* he called to Myra.

Myra smiled. The driver knelt down the bus down with a *beep beep beep* noise, so she wouldn't have to step so high. She stepped on board. "Just going downtown. Fortunately, I didn't have to wait *too* long, thanks!" said Myra to the driver.

"You're welcome. So, you're really going to try to go out in this snow? You have a lot of courage", laughed the driver.

"You can't let a little bit of snow stop you!" said Myra. She sat down near the driver to get her bus fare from her coin pouch. She looked in her purse, but the red coin pouch was not there. She knew she had checked for it before she left. She searched inside her bag. She pulled some things out and laid them down by her side. She still couldn't find her coin pouch. Now, she was becoming concerned. The driver started again down the crusty ice road, smiling sweetly. Myra felt for the plastic coin pouch and finally felt it. She grabbed it and pulled out her red coin pouch. The red coin pouch was now *gray!* She heard a high-pitched noise in her ears. She noticed something else. Her red knit mittens were gray, also. Myra looked around. Something was strange, *something was not right*. She tugged at her red knit shawl and saw that it was yellow, too. Myra froze. She'd heard about stroke victims seeing strange colors just before a stroke happened. Myra's heart pounded. *She was having a stroke!*

She put her things back in the purse and sat there, her arms clutching her purse to her chest, and waited for the stroke, terrified. She turned her head and looked around the bus. There was an old man and a mother with two kids on the bus. They didn't seem to notice Myra. Her heart pounded with fear. She closed her eyes tight, opened them again. Her mittens were still gray. She wanted to get off the bus, but that would put her in the middle of nowhere, in the snow. Myra waited for the expected blackout. She didn't want to cry out to anyone. She waited, her eyes shut tight, her mouth taut… but nothing happened. She remembered that she still had to give the driver her bus fare. She looked at the driver, but he seemed concerned with something else. His sweet smile was now gone, replaced by a look of puzzlement.

Suddenly, he pulled the bus over and stopped. He turned on the red Emergency blinkers. He opened the door, got out and walked to the right side of the road. Myra looked out the side window and saw the bus driver slowly approaching the stop sign at the intersection. The formerly red stop sign was now pale gray. The driver got up close to the sign, looked close, felt the cold metal sign. He heard a high-pitched squeal in his head. *"Something's not right here."* he said. He looked around. On the next corner, he could see the next stop sign, and it was pale gray, too! He wheeled around, looking up and down. The sky was still a pearly gray, like it had been for several weeks. The sun had rarely been seen. Spokane had not been able to see the Boes-Stilmaker comet because of eternally cloudy skies. The driver noticed that the trees, or what little showed of them, were *blue*. He squinted, shook his head. Something was wrong with the color of things, but he didn't know what. *Gray stop signs? Was this some kind of joke? Who did this?* He looked around, half-expecting to camera crews rush out and tell him he had been the victim of a prank. But there was no camera crew. He suddenly wondered about something. Quickly, he crunched back to the rear of the bus to check his red emergency lights. They were now gray emergency lights. "Something is *definitely* not right, here" he said. He wheeled around, looking at vehicles parked on the side. *All their red brake-lights were gray!* Every car had gray brake-light lenses instead of red. There were no red-painted cars in sight either, although he wasn't aware of it yet.

Myra was relieved when she saw the bus driver peering at the gray "STOP" sign. She was not having a stroke. *He* saw the red thing turn gray, too. Myra calmed down. The Mexican mother with her two kids looked around, not sure what was happening. *"Donde esta rojo, mama?"* said one of the kids. The old man leaned forward, watching the bus driver outside. The bus driver got back on board. He smiled sweetly smile at the passengers and said, "Excuse me, folks, we're going to be a few minutes late… something is definitely *wrong* going on around here… gonna have to radio in."

"They makin' gray stop signs now?" asked the old man.

---

It was as if the Color Spectrum Coach had to make some last-minute cuts to the team:

"All right, you guys settle down, enough of the horseplay! Settle Down. Before I start, I just wanna thank you all for coming out and trying out this spring. We gotta make some cuts. I wanna let the guys who are cut know that it wasn't because of any lack of abilities, but because of unforeseen events, we gotta make these cuts. What's so funny Blue, you think this is funny? You wanna take a lap? All right, then. Now, the following hues, tints and saturations are cut: Red, you're cut. You, Orange, you're cut. Scarlet, cut. Vermilion, out. Burgundy, you're cut, sorry. Cerise, cut. Crimson, out. Carmine, arrivederci, you're cut. Puce, cut. *I said it's not funny, Blue, go take a lap!* That goes for *you too, Green!* Yellow, you wanna get cut? Keep it up. Brown, you're cut, but I wanna let you know it was close, we like you and want you to come back next year. Purple, you're cut, sorry. Violet, you're cut. Maroon, you're cut. Ochre, cut. Rust, out, you're a tough boy and we'd like to see you back. Dusty Rose, cut. That's all for now. We wanna thank all those again, for coming out and trying out, we like you, you're all tough boys, and we wanna see you guys back at tryouts next year. Now, all you Bozos who made the team, get out there and take a lap!"

---

The boys were out on the City golf course, hacking and duffering and drinking and flirting with the scantily clad Tee Girls, who provided liquid refreshment at every other tee. These guys were the real die-hards of the course. Stan, Greg, Dave and Red were up at the starter shack at daybreak every day, rain or shine. They were all military vets with cast-iron stomachs. They could down quarts and quarts of Vodka and Gin like nothing. They were the best of golf buddies. They were like happy lumbering bears, laughing, roaring and joking. Sometimes they even managed to put the little ball in the hole.

All four were on the eleventh green, putting out. It was Stan's turn. He tapped it towards the hole and missed. "What's wrong, Stan, can't get it in the hole? Hahahahaha!" The other three laughed. Stan just looked at them. "Is that the best you can come up with? That joke is old as the mountains and twice as moldy!" He got set and tapped again. He missed again. The guys laughed. "All right, all right, shaddup, you guys!" He got set again. He was about to tap, when the green turned blue. Stan heard a high pitched noise in his head. He was frozen in putting position. "What the hell?"

"What's going on?" The grass turned blue. "Jesus what's happening?"

"What's that noise? Do you hear something?" The sky turned green. "Stan, are you OK? Look at him, his face turned gray!" They looked at each other. They were all gray colored. They dropped their putters and wheeled around looking up and down and each other. "Oh, my God!"

"What is that, smog?"

"It looks like green smoke in the sky!" Stan remained frozen in putting position, puzzled. Suddenly, he felt sharp pain in his chest and arms. He looked up at the sky, then at the others. "I don't feel very good, guys." He fell flat on his back on the blue green. "Stan! Stan!"

"Call 911! Call 911! He's having a heart attack!"

"I think I'm having one, too!" said Red. He sat down.

"I called 911, all I get is a busy signal."

"Try it again."

"What's happening? What's that noise?"

"Jesus Christ, Stan's *dead!*"

"Red! Red! Are ya all right?" Red shook his head. "I… think so…" He stood up and then fell down, passing out. "Red! Help! Help, somebody! Help us!" shouted Dave. The scantily clad Tee girls were screaming, looking at each other. Their flesh was gray. They ran towards the Clubhouse, screaming, and Greg and Dave followed them, shouting for help.

---

Doggins prepared to take Sugar and Shep out for their walk, like he did every day, rain or shine. He was always taking dogs out for walks. He was a professional dog walker. Doggins was not his real name, but the name of his dog walking service in Seattle. It was painted on his business van. His real name was Bill. Business was good for Bill, and he had many clients.

Doggins' dogs today were, Shep, a German Shepherd and Sugar, a Springer spaniel. He covered all his dogs with a day-glo orange jacket so cars would see them. He also wore the same color vest so he could be seen as well. He put harnesses on them and attached the leashes to their shoulders, so they wouldn't hurt their necks if they were suddenly lurched. Off they went, down the suburban tree-lined street. The dogs were a bit older than most, and they padded gingerly down the hill, looking to the left and right, enjoying the sights of other dogs, cats, squirrels and people. The street was secluded, with not much traffic. Doggins always walked his dogs on the right side of the road.

It was a sunny, but hazy late afternoon day. The shadows lengthened fast. Doggins never walked dogs at night, so this would be the last walk of the day. He was heading for Doggy park so the dogs could greet other dogs and play for a few minutes. He wondered why it was so hazy outside. He looked up at the pine trees. They looked strangely blue colored at the tops of the trees. Suddenly, he heard a high-pitched noise in his ears. The dogs heard it too. All of them looked around. Doggins noticed that the hazy sky was now *green*. He looked at the trees. They were blue. So was the grass on people's lawns. *"What the heck?"* The dogs stopped. Shep started barking and Sugar started keening, as if she were in pain. Shep wouldn't stop barking. "Shep!" yelled Doggins. Shep growled and turned to Sugar, who was still whining. All of a sudden, Shep attacked Sugar biting her viciously. It was a full scale dog fight. Shep easily got Sugar down on her back, biting her and snarling, tearing at her long fur. Doggins pulled Shep off Sugar and lurching back. Shep lurched back on the leash and went at Sugar again. Doggins was shocked. Shep was a normally sweet dog. But now, he was attacking Sugar savagely, for no apparent reason. "Shep! Shep! *Radat!*" Radat meant nothing in particular. It was just a vocal command to heel, that dogs seemed to understand. But it didn't work on Shep this time. Shep was still tearing at poor Sugar, who yelped and keened in pain. Doggins pulled Shep off and back from Sugar again, but Shep lurched back, and the leash handle came out of Doggins hand. Shep ran back at Sugar, who was limping away. Shep caught her and tore at her again. He was killing her. Seeing that she wouldn't last much longer, Doggins ran up to the fighting dogs and grabbed Shep by the collar, pulling him off Sugar. Shep turned and bit Doggins on his arm. Doggins yelled in pain and let go Shep. Sugar ran away, badly wounded. *"RADAT! RADAT!"* he shouted at Shep. This time, it worked. Shep heeled. Doggins picked up the leash. He looked at his arm. It was gray colored and there was yellow blood coming out of the bite wound! *"What in the world?"* The high-pitched tone was still in his ears. "Come on, Shep!" he ordered, wondering what he was going to say to the owners of the dogs. Shep just stood there. He wouldn't budge. "Shep!" Shep turned around and snarled at Doggins, viciously. "Shep! What's wrong with you?" Shep started growling at Doggins. He advanced on him a few steps. "Shep! RADAT!" Shep snarled, baring his sharp white canines to Doggins. The fur on his back was standing on end in a ridge. He advanced a couple more steps. *"RADAT!*

*RADAT!"* Shep was coming at Doggins now. Doggins dropped the leash and turned and ran, but Shep easily caught up with him and pushed him down and got him by the neck. His vice-grip jaws closed tight.

---

Woody was flying in his twin engine Cessna near Catalina Island. He was a seasoned pilot with many flight hours logged. He flew every weekend. Sometimes his wife Sandy would accompany him, but not very often. She was afraid of heights. Woody looked down on the blue Ocean. It was a sunny day, but strangely hazy. The haze appeared to be high above the white clouds. He circled over the island and Avalon Harbor. He noted the infamous Catalina Island landing strip, with it's sometimes dangerous bumpy runway. He'd landed many times there, with no problems. He radioed in for clearance to land. When he received confirmation, he banked right and headed in. As he turned, he noticed that something was not right. The hazy sky turned green! He suddenly heard a deafening, high-pitched squeal in his head. He was stunned. He stared at the sky. He was confused. He lost his sense of direction. The squealing was very loud. He reached for his radio mike and pushed the button. "I… I… umm… I'm…" He couldn't find words to say, couldn't speak. He didn't know what he was doing anymore. The radio blared. "Unidentified aircraft please identify yourself!" He just stared at the mike. "Unidentified aircraft, please respond!" He pushed the button. "I'm in the sky and the sky is green… I… I…I'm not…" He pulled back on the wheel and went upwards. Up, up, up, he went not realizing what he was doing. His plane was vertical and his engines cut out. He dropped like a rock, going into a death-spiral that he would not be able to pull out of. He wondered why the ocean was emerald green as he plummeted down, down, down. He stared in wonderment as he hit the water.

# CHAPTER 21

## The Red Seer

**M**IKEY CALLED IKEY, who was head of security deep down in the vaults beneath Martin Boes Aerodynamics. Ikey was a black man like Mikey. They were good friends and lived near each other and would often visit each other's families. Mikey worked twelve hour shifts five days a week in the vaults. The vaults held Martin Boes most important formulas and collector items that he did not have on display in the spacious main office. Formulas for Ice That Wouldn't Melt, X-Ray Crayons and Zipgun Gelpels were locked up securely in coded vials that only Martin Boes could read. Ikey answered the phone. "Vaults."

"Hey Ike, it's Mike."

"Mike! What's up, Cuz?"

"Not sure. Did you get that alarm?"

"I sure did! The boss called and told me to stand by. What's going on?"

"I don't know for sure. Something weird. I can't explain it, but the colors of things are off. I wanted to ask you. Do you see any unusual changes in color down there?"

"What? Color changes? No. What do you mean?"

"I mean, do you see everything in its usual color? Have your eyes been affected in any way?"

"No. the colors are all the same, as usual. Did they drop a bomb up there?"

"No, nothing like that. Everything's the same except for the colors. I can't explain it. The colors are all wrong." Ikey shrugged. "Colors are fine down here. I'm looking around… computer's working fine, I see all colors fine."

"Can you see red?"

"Red? Sure, I see red fine… I'm looking at the apple Regina packed in my lunch. Still looks red to me. Are you pulling my leg?"

"Ike, you know I never joke around. Now, look at your hands. What color are they?"

"My hands? They're brown, like always. What color *would* they be?"

"Would you please look in the mirror?" Ikey walked over to the mirror. "I'm looking at the man in the mirror, my friend!"

"And what do you see in the mirror?"

"I see a handsome devil and an employee who needs a raise. *What* is going on, Mike?"

"I'm coming down there. See you in a few."

Mikey took the long elevator down to the vaults. Since Ikey said that he could see red, Mikey figured his color vision would return to normal once he got down to the vaults. When the big door opened and Ikey greeted him, Mikey received a jolt. Ikey was dark gray color with blue veins webbing his face. His eye sockets appeared dark blue. Mikey just stood there, staring at Ikey. "Are you all right, Mike?"

"Uh, yeah. Ike, do I look OK? You see anything wrong with me?"

"No, you're just as ugly as you ever were. What are you talking about?" Mikey entered the vaults and looked at the computer monitor. He saw that blue was green and green was blue, and he could see no red. His descent into the sunless depths had not restored his color vision. He was very disappointed. He wheeled about, trying to see if his vision would improve. It didn't. "Now tell me the truth, Ike, do I look OK to you? Can you see colors normally?"

"Sure, man. I haven't seen anything different since the alarms went off. The boss wouldn't tell me what was wrong."

"There's some kind of smoggy haze outside. The worst smog, ever. Super smog…" Mikey's cell phone chimed. "Speak of the Devil" he said, noting his caller ID. "This is Mike."

"Mike, did you go down to the vaults, yet? asked Martin Boes.

"Yes sir, I'm down here now."

"Can you see red? Can you see normal colors down there?"

"No sir, I'm sorry, I can't. I thought sure I'd be able to, but I can't. It made no difference." There was a long pause. Mikey could sense his disappointment.

"I'm very sorry to hear that. I thought the same thing. You're certain about this?"

"Yes sir." Ikey noticed a tear in Mikey's eye. "But, sir! Ike says he can see normal colors."

"He did? He can? Is he there? Please let me speak to him!" Mikey handed Ikey the phone without looking at him. Ikey was now very concerned. "What's wrong, brother?" Mikey looked at his gray-blue face. "Boss wants to talk to you."

"Yes sir, this is Dwight."

"Dwight, is there anyone else down there that hasn't come topside since the alarms went off?"

"No sir, I'm the only one down here. Mike is here, but he came down a few minutes ago."

"Is everything OK in the vaults?"

"Yes sir! Everything's A-OK, down here. I made the rounds several times just to make sure. Uh, what happened up there, sir?"

"I'm not sure, but there has been some kind of major atmospheric change. There's some kind of haze or smog that changed the color of things. Everyone is color blind!"

"Everybody is… *color blind*, you say, sir?"

"I know it sounds crazy, Dwight. I'm still waiting for more info on this. But right now, I would like to ask you to stay down there and not come up until I get down there. Mike tells me your color vision is normal, is that right?"

"Yes sir! I'm looking at a red apple right now, and it's red."

"Great! So it looks like the people who are underground weren't affected by the color change. I want you and Mike to stay below until I get there. I need to talk with you about something. I'll be down there in two hours."

"Yes sir. We'll stay put down here."

"Thank you, Dwight." He hung up. Ikey handed the phone back to Mikey, who was still dazed and confused. He was not used to the new color changes. "So! Everybody's color blind, topside?"

"Yup. Me, too. I thought if I came down here, my vision would come back. It didn't." He looked Ikey in the face, and then turned away. It was hard to look at him. "Why are you looking at me like that? What do I look like to you?"

"A zombie. You look to me like a zombie. Your skin is olive green, and you have blue veins all over your face." Ikey's eyes widened. He started laughing. "You gotta be kidding! This is a joke, right?"

"No joke. You know I don't make jokes." Ikey rushed over to the mirror and peered at himself. "I sure don't see it. You wanna look in the mirror?"

"I've seen it. I've seen what I look like. I'm olive green, too."

"So, how come I can see red, and you can't?"

"I don't know. Maybe the boss can explain it. I know

it had something to do with the comet the other day. It did... something."

"Well. Let's get some chow, I'm hungry. You want a beer?"

"Right now, I could use a forty."


Two hours later, Martin Boes arrived at the underground vault. He was color blind, just like everyone else. He was extra careful while driving, because his depth perception was off, and there were no visible red lights. Stop signs and traffic lights were pale yellow. The sky was green. Trees, grass and bushes were blue. As he descended to the underground vault, he hoped and prayed his color vision would return, once he got down, out of sunlight. It was not to be. The big door opened, and there was Mikey and Ikey. They were both olive green, to the eyes of Martin Boes. "What happened, boss?" asked Mikey. "Star Dust." replied Martin Boes.

"Star Dust?"

"Or rather, comet dust. Dust from the tail of the comet has permeated the upper atmosphere. It seems to have distorted the human visual color spectrum. It must have seeped through the hole in the ozone layer at the North Pole." He looked around the vaults, trying to find traces of red. There were none to be seen. "As a result, everybody has gone color blind!"

"Everyone? You mean everybody in town?" Martin Boes sadly shook his head. "No. I mean everybody, everywhere. All of us. The whole country. *The whole world*. I called Professor Stilmaker. He's confirmed what I said. It's... terrible! Something terrible has happened"

"But sir! How come I can see colors?" said Ikey. "How come I'm not color blind? Is it because I was down here?"

"Exactly. You're down here in artificial light. Your eyes and vision were not affected. People who work or live underground, such as miners, or the folks at NORAD and SAC, don't seem to be affected. But there's a catch. It seems that those underground who emerge into sunlight are turned color blind. Their vision does not return to normal when they go back underground. They become color blind, too."

"That's crazy!" said Ikey. "Do you mean that if I go topside, I'll go color blind, too?"

"Yes, that's my understanding. It's still too early to tell for sure. Is there any way to lower the lights down here?"

"We can shut down most of the lights."

"Do that for me please, Mike? I want to try something." Mike went to the control panel and switched off all the lights, except for two. They were all silhouetted in the low lights. "Is that OK, sir?"

"Yes, that's fine." Martin Boes looked around the vaults, as if searching for something. He found what he was looking for. He picked up Ikey's apple. In the darkness, he could see traces of red in the apple. "Mike, look at this apple. Can you see red?" Mike peered at the apple for a few seconds. "Yes! Yes sir! I can see red. Well, a little bit… not much."

"But you do see *some* red, don't you?"

"Yes sir. Definitely. But it's so dark…"

"Interesting! You can turn up the lights, again." Mikey did so, and red disappeared again. "Can you still see red, Dwight?"

"Yes sir. No change at all."

"Good. Now, I'd like to discuss something with you, Dwight. Right now, you have normal vision. But, if you go topside, there is a very good chance you will become color blind. You most likely will *not* regain normal vision. I need someone who can see red, to help me in finding a solution to this problem. A *Red Seer*, as it were. You are that Red Seer, Dwight. I want to ask you to stay down here in the vaults for the time being, until the dust in the upper atmosphere settles. Hopefully, this won't last very long. If you choose to stay down here, I'll install living quarters for you and your family. You'll be paid for every hour you are down here, along with your regular salary. And I'll give you that much deserved raise I know you wanted. If you choose to go topside, you'll lose your color vision. I'll think none the worse of you if you decide to go up. The choice is yours." Mikey was entranced. "Hunh… a Red Seer. I guess that makes me a very important person!"

"Yes, it does. Right now, you are one of the most important people in the world."

"But I have to stay down here? For how long?"

"I'm not exactly sure. It's still too early to tell. Of course, you can emerge any time you want, if you so decide. I need someone who can see red."

"And I can have anything I want while I'm down here?" Martin Boes smiled. "Sure you can. Within reason, of course."

"I'll do it, sir. I'll stay down here for the duration. I'll be your Red Seer."

"Thank you, Dwight. Much appreciated. You'll be an extremely valuable asset to the company and Boes-Soleil. I'll arrange for living quarters and pay all your expenses. I must speak with Professor Stilmaker, now. Notify your wife and family. I'll give you a call tonight. Thank you again, Dwight, you are a true soldier!"

"You're welcome, sir!" And Martin Boes shook hands with Ikey, knowing that it might take a long time for *this* dust to settle, if it did at all. It might take a long, long, time.

# CHAPTER 22

## Change You Never Expected

THE PRESIDENT OF the United States was about to hold a color-blind, nationally-televised Emergency Presidential Address concerning the disruption of the color spectrum and the ensuing color changes caused by the *Boes-Stilmaker Comet*. The President stood on the cue mark for the camera test, chatting with the crew and make-up artists, who could only dab yellowish powder on the President's face to cover up blotches; the President appeared gray with dark blue shading, just like everybody else. He had no flesh color. Neither did the First Lady, his children and relatives. Neither did the Joint Chiefs of Staff. Neither did all the members of the Senate and Congress. Neither did the Chief Justices, nor the Judges. Neither did the Pages and Interns. The President of the United States could not see red, either, just like everyone else. And to the President of the United States, green was now blue and blue was now green, just as it now was to everyone else.

He was a color-blind President, about to address a color-blind nation, in a color-blind world. This would be a historically important and unforgettable speech, unprecedented in history. This was one time were there would be no dissent.

He had endured much recent criticism for what was viewed as a slow response to an oil spill disaster and his handling of the economy. This was one time that a President would be able to give a *really* monumental speech without fear of disagreement and heckling. This was something shared with everybody on Earth. This was something Congress, the Senate, Democrats, Republicans, Moderates, the Radical Left, Tea Party Conservatives, Knee-jerk Liberals, Independents, Ultra-Right Alarmists and Anarchists would all degree upon: *"No Red. Not a good thing!"* The President began his speech:

"My fellow Americans! I come before you all tonight to inform you and to calm and reassure you about the recent, unprecedented events caused by the close brush with the Boes-Stilmaker Comet. As you know by now, there has been *change*- an unexpected change. A change in the way we all see color. For instance, what was once green now appears blue, and what was once blue now appears green. But the most significant and important change you will notice, is the absence of the color *Red*. When the Boes-Stilmaker Comet brushed by the Earth, various chemicals and elements in the tail of the comet distorted the wavelengths of the human visual color spectrum, resulting in the changes you now see. We are not alone. The color spectrum distortion is a *world-wide phenomena*. Every human being on the planet is affected by the color distortion. The tremendous, sweeping tail of the comet has engulfed the Earth. Gas, ice and dust particles trapped in the atmosphere have distorted the human visual color wavelengths, causing these color changes. We are still within the tail of the comet, and will continue to be for quite some time. I urge every American and every citizen on Earth not to panic. For what was once considered Blue is still indeed Blue- it only appears Green. And what was once considered Green is still indeed Green- it only appears Blue. And *Red?* I want to emphasize that Red is still there- it just cannot be seen at this time.

This is a completely unexpected event, unprecedented in all

recorded human history. No one would ever conceive that the entire planet would be struck color-blind. Unfortunately, that is just what happened. Your President and his administration have reacted speedily to this crisis. I have authorized emergency government funding to adapt to the color changes throughout the United States and its territories. We are working together with all nations in adapting to these changes, which, I am told are temporary. There is hope. Our leading scientists and astrophysicists state that there is a high probability that the color spectrum will return to normal after the tail of the comet recedes and dissipates. For the time being, we can, and we *must* persevere through these changes. We are already adapting to these color changes in our immediate life. Our nation's flag, "Old Glory" has been changed by the event. *Red,* the color representing Courage and the *blood* of those who gave their lives for our country, has been eradicated. Therefore, I have authorized a temporary change in the design of the American flag." At this point, a large screen behind the president revealed the new flag design. "Here is the temporary, Provisional Flag of the United States of America. It is a field of dark blue with fifty-six stars representing the fifty states and its territories. It is basically the upper left portion of our nation's previous flag, extended full-length. This is intended to be only a temporary flag, in waiting for the day when the color Red returns to us, and our beloved "Old Glory" will wave proudly, once again." He turned to the camera. When will this happen, you ask? The answer at this time is still not certain. For the time being, we are all affected by the color changes. Everyone, around the world, shares your affliction. Everyone- the young, the old, the rich, the poor. I myself, your President am also affected, along with my wife and children. The world is united in their handicap in this unprecedented disaster, like a lace that runs through everyone and everything. Let us *stay* united in our faith that this is only a *temporary* discomfort, a *short term nuisance* that will eventually fade away.

Can we, as a nation, survive living with green skies? *Yes, we can!*

Can we, as a nation, survive living with blue trees and grass? *Yes, we can!*

Can we, as a nation, survive living without the color *Red? Yes, we can!*

It may take some time. It may be difficult. It may be distressing and tedious. But the American people have always been strong during times of crises, have always adapted to unexpected events. This will be a true test of courage, without the presence of the color Red. Again, I urge every American to stay calm and be strong. We will update you on current atmospheric conditions as reports come in. Every soul on Earth can be united in their hopes and expectations that the true color spectrum will return, and soon. Thank you, Good Night, and May God Bless Us All."

There was no Republican rebuttal to the President's speech, or from anyone else. No reporters shouted hurried questions at the president as he left the podium. People were still in shock, though they wouldn't admit it. Questions would be asked, later. But if there were any dissenters, their response would probably have been something along the lines of:

"The President is wrong. He is only attempting to minimize the seriousness of this catastrophe. Without the color Red, human depth perception is virtually destroyed. Every aspect of our lives has been disrupted. Our appearance is ghastly. And what about our enemies, those who seek to do us harm? Will *they* use the loss of the color Red to gain a military advantage? What about *that*, Mr. President?" And they would be justified in asking these questions.

# CHAPTER 23

## To The Uglification of All

JIMBO AND BREN stood naked looking at each other in their bedroom. They were pale and ghastly. Their skin was a translucent pale gray and had greenish blue blood veins showing over every square inch of their bodies. Bren's lush red hair now had a gray, dirty blonde, dish-water appearance. Her blue eyes were now green. It appeared as if she had two black eyes from a fight. Her lips and nipples were the same color as her skin. Her breasts were spider-webbed with veins not normally apparent when red was there. Under strong lights, she could vaguely see her own insides through her opaque, translucent skin. Jimbo's skin was a bit darker, so he had blue-green shading with his gray skin. His brown hair appeared dark olive color with dirty blonde highlights. His face sported teal blood veins, most apparent at his forehead and temple. He also had the double black eyes, around his new blue eyes. (His eyes were green colored before the comet arrived) Jimbo could see his guts, too. They stared at each other naked for five minutes before Jimbo spoke. "Honey, you look like hell!" he said. Always the joker, no matter what.

"You're not exactly Mel Gibson, either!" They both

laughed, but not much. Jimbo did have a Mel Gibson kind of rugged look before the taking of Red. Now, he looked like an angry, Mel Gibson zombie! And Bren looked like an angry, Mel Gibson zombie wife! "Well! *This* is a helluva deal!" remarked Jimbo. How did we get so ugly? How did everybody get so ugly?"

"It said on the news that that comet messed up the color spectrum when it went by. It polluted the atmosphere." replied Bren. "Now everyone's color-blind, especially to Red. They said everybody looks like this!" It was the same with their kids. Their skin was pale gray with green shading. Both had their own pair of double black eyes, like everyone else. Jodie's long red hair was now dirty dish-water gray. Her blue eyes were now green. Her boobs that Harold liked so much were now spider-webbed with repulsive veins. Her Red leather diary that held the logistics of her make-out sessions was now gray. Her pink and red clothes were now dingy, pale gray. She gave new meaning to the expression *Ewwwww!* when she looked in the mirror. Josh's red hair was now dingy gray. His previously green eyes were now blue. His lips and gums were gray, like everyone else in the world. His red plastic toothbrush that he cherished had gray, though it was as useful as ever. The whole family tried to visit their doctor, but was turned away, because he had his own problems. He looked like a ghastly zombie, too. They tried to visit the Optometrist about their not being able to see Red, but were turned away, because the eye doctor could not see Red, either. Nobody could. With the absence of the color Red, all human skin appeared pale gray with either blue or green shading depending on how dark their skin was before the taking of Red. Darker skinned people actually fared better than the lighter skinned people, because their skin appeared dark blue-gray, with the unsightly veins not as apparent. But everybody was *ugly!* It was mass *uglification!* Everybody was equal in their ugliness. Even the beauteous Soleil, Martin Boes' sometime girlfriend, suffered the humiliation of being *uglified*.

No one escaped. Bren looked at herself naked in the full length mirror. "God, I'm ugly!"

"Come here, ugly!" said Jimbo, walking across the room and embracing Bren. They kissed and hugged deeply. "You may be ugly, but you're still *my* ugly!" They kissed and felt each other up, standing there naked. They closed their eyes. Their bodies still felt the same. There was nothing different, except for visuals. They felt, rubbed and caressed each other. Soon, they were getting hot. "How about us ugly people hit the sack?" suggested Jimbo. Bren was relieved. She was afraid Jimbo would be turned off by her appearance. "You… want to? Should we?

"What else is there to do?" he chortled." Jimbo took her hand and led her to the bed. "This is weird! I can't look at you like this" said Bren, with tears in her eyes. "Maybe if you kind of squint your eyes it'll be better" said Jimbo, helpfully. They tried it. "Never mind, it doesn't work… but we can always turn off the lights!" chuckled Jim. They did. They went to bed in darkness. In the darkness, some said, a hint of red could be seen. In total darkness, Red was there, but since it was total darkness, still could not be seen. They made love, and their sex was as good as it ever was, because of their love and faith in each other during and after the taking of Red.

Red was gone, and there was nothing to be done about it. They couldn't re-create Red, simply because *it could not be seen!* The Earth was trapped in the tail of the comet, trapped like a bug in amber. There was nothing anybody on Earth could do about it. It was just too bad, for Earth. Tough titty. *"Tough titty, said the kitty, when the milk went dry"* as the children's verse went. There was a New Order of Colors, now. It was Yellow, Blue and Green. The dust trapped in the upper atmosphere was going to be there for some time. The top twelve Earth scientists and astrophysicists, led by Professor Stilmaker, affably shrugged their shoulders in unison in a *"that's the way it goes!"* manner. Computers weren't the answer. They couldn't bring back red. All the supercomputers were useless toys, in this respect. All the money thrown at the problem would be useless. Money could do nothing about it. Suspected terrorists could not be blamed for this. There were no evil, diabolical super villain masterminds behind this. This wasn't the movies. There were no super-human beings with powers enough to do anything about it. Vampires, if they actually existed, would have been at an extreme disadvantage at not seeing Red, and would have been as helpless as anyone. No wizards could chant and wave a magic wand and make Red come back. No man in an iron-clad, jet-propelled flying suit could do anything about it. No individual with spider-like capabilities could do anything about it, although he *could* scamper up the sides of the gray brick buildings, if he wanted to. No Hobbit could drop a powerful ring into a fiery pit to bring back Red. No super-powered man wearing colorful tights and a cape, even if he flew around the world quickly and repeatedly in an effort to turn back time, could bring back Red.

# CHAPTER 24

## The Ring

STILMAKER LOST HIS solid gold wedding ring, somewhere, sometime just after the taking of Red. It meant very much to Stilmaker, who had been married to Bambi for forty-five years. He always had it before, and never lost it before. The ring was part of him, part of his body, and part of his soul. The taking of Red had confused and befuddled him so much, that he was not himself. He was trying to adjust to no red, like everybody else, but it was beginning to affect him in unusual ways. Up until now, he was sharp and still level-headed at seventy-three. But when he lost his ring, he went slightly nuts.

"First I go color-blind, and now this!" he moaned. His wife Bambi hugged and kissed him, telling him that it was just a ring. "No, I'm sorry, dear, that was not *just a ring*. That ring was part of *me* and part of *you*." he moped. "I still have my ring', she said, raising her finger. "Don't worry about it! We can get you another one. *I'll* get you another one."

"No, you won't. That ring was irreplaceable. You might as well get me a heart transplant to replace my broken one. It's gone… gone like Red… maybe I'll find it somewhere." Bambi was touched by the way he felt. "Let's go lie down and talk about it." They retreated to their plush down-feather bed.

The next day, Stilmaker was at Manny's having a Reuben Sandwich with his usual split-pea soup. They still had not found a way to make green pea soup not look blue, so his pea soup was still blue. It still tasted the same, it was just blue. He was watching the Dodgers on the big screen. The Dodgers had adjusted their uniform colors back to blue from green. Instead of the red numbers on their uniforms, they wore black numbers. But the blue seats and blue pavilions were still green; they were still not adjusted after Red was taken away. The waitress came up to Stilmaker. "Professor Stilmaker, I have something for you." She held out his big gold ring in her hand.

"My ring!" His eyes widened like a little boy. "My ring!" He swallowed the bite of his sandwich. "Oh My Gah! You found my ring! Oh, God!" Tears filled his eyes. He took his ring and held it close, peering through the tears of joy. My Gah! How… where did you ever find it?"

"I didn't find it, sir. The dishwasher found it in a bowl of soup. He turned it in." It was true. Sometime after the taking of Red, his ring slipped off and dropped into his pea soup he was having that day. The dishwasher could have easily gotten three hundred dollars for that ring, but he was honest enough to turn it in. He had a gold wedding band, too. "I… I can't thank you enough for returning my ring. Is that gentleman here, the one who found my ring?"

"Yes, he's here now. Would you like to speak to him?"

"Yes, yes! I want to thank him, please ask him to come out" The waitress nodded and went to the kitchen. A minute later, she returned with the dishwasher. "This is Raoul. He found your ring." Stilmaker leaped to his feet, throwing out his big paw to the shy dishwasher. "God bless you, Raoul! Thank you so much for returning my ring. It meant so much to me!" He shook Raoul's hand, practically crushing it in his big ham fist. He wouldn't let go. "I feel alive again! Here!" Stilmaker reached into his pocket and pulled out his Sterling silver bill-fold. He peeled off a fifty dollar bill and handed it to Raoul. Raoul politely refused, but Stilmaker grabbed his hand with an iron grip and pressed the fifty into his palm. "Much appreciated, my friend!" he said looking at Raoul level in the eyes. Raoul accepted the fifty with a shy smile."And if you ever need anything, *anything*, just come and see me! I'm Professor Stilmaker."

"Thank you, sir!" said Raoul, and he went back to work.

"And you, young lady! You don't get away so easy! He peeled off another fifty and handed it to the waitress. "Oh, Professor, I didn't do anything to deserve this."

*"Hup bup bup bup bup*! Not a word! I won't hear about it! You brought back my ring!" he pressed the fifty into her palm. "With many thanks" he said, tenderly. The waitress thanked him and went back to work. Stilmaker was elated. Replenished, he finished his Reuben and blue pea soup, ignoring the Dodgers, all the while with his eyes on his beloved ring. He didn't want to lose it again! He put the ring on his finger. He was whole again! He took it off, held it in his big hand, adoring it. He felt the old vibrations, the love he shared, the power of his beloved ring. He called back the waitress.

"Yes, Professor?"

"I… I can't thank you enough for returning my ring. Is that gentleman here, the one who found my ring?"

"Uh, yes sir, he was just—"

"Yes, yes, I want to thank him, please ask him to come out." The waitress paused, nodded and went to the kitchen. A minute later, she returned with the dishwasher. Stilmaker leaped to his feet again and held out his big paw. The dishwasher took it again and shook, uncertainly. "Was it you that found my ring? God Bless you, my boy! And what is your name?"

"Raoul, sir… did I not just…"

"God bless you, Raoul! Thank you so much for returning

my ring. It meant so much to me!" He shook Raoul's hand again, practically crushing it in his big ham fist. He wouldn't let go. "I feel alive again! Here!" Stilmaker reached into his pocket and pulled out his Sterling silver bill-fold. He peeled off a fifty dollar bill and handed it to Raoul. Raoul tried to explain that he had already met him, but Stilmaker grabbed his hand with an iron grip and pressed the fifty into his palm. "Much appreciated my friend!" he said looking at Raoul level in the eyes. Raoul accepted the fifty with a shy smile. "And if you ever need anything, *anything*, just come and see me! I'm Professor Stilmaker"

"Thank you, sir!" said Raoul, smiling politely and looking at the waitress, he went back to work. "And you, young lady! You don't get away so easy..." He peeled off another fifty and handed it to the waitress. "But Professor, don't you remember? You just..."

"*Hup bup bup bup bup!* Not a word! I don't want to hear about it! You brought back my ring!" he pressed the fifty into her palm. "With many thanks" he said, tenderly. The waitress took the fifty. She didn't want to hurt his feelings. Stilmaker finished lunch, leaving another fifty dollar bill for a tip. He felt enlivened, replenished, renewed. He was light as a feather. He waltzed out of Manny's with a new look on life in a world without red. As he waltzed outside, a guy came up to him. "Sir? Sir? Would you give me a dollar for a sandwich?"

"Maybe, but I'd have to *see* the sandwich, first", said Stilmaker, waltzing away.

# CHAPTER 25

Stardust (or How to Go From Trichromatic
to Dichromatic in One Easy Step)

COLOR VISION IS the capacity of a human being to distinguish objects based on the wavelengths or frequencies of the light they reflect, emit, or transmit. The nervous system derives color by comparing the responses to light from the several types of cone receptors in the eye. These cone photoreceptors are sensitive to different portions of the visible spectrum. For humans, the visible spectrum ranges approximately from 380 to 740 nm, and there are three types of cones.

A "red" apple does not emit red light. Rather, it simply absorbs all the frequencies of visible light shining on it except for a group of frequencies that is perceived as red, which are reflected. An apple is perceived to be red only because the human eye can distinguish between different wavelengths.

Perception of color is achieved in mammals through color receptors containing pigments with different spectral sensitivities. In most primates closely related to humans there are three types of color receptors (cone cells). This is known as trichromatic color vision, so these primates, like humans, are known as *trichromats*. Other primates and mammals are known as *dichromats*, and some mammals have little or no color vision at all. The evolution of trichromatic vision in primates occurred as the ancestors of modern monkeys, apes, and humans switched from diurnal (daytime) activity and began consuming fruits and leaves from flowering plants. Many species can see wavelengths that fall outside the visible spectrum. Bees and many other insects can see light in the ultraviolet, which helps them find nectar in flowers. Birds too, can see into the ultraviolet (300-400 nm), and some have sex-dependant markings on their plumage, which are only visible in the ultraviolet range.

Colors that can be produced by visible light of a single wavelength are referred to as pure spectral colors. Although the color spectrum is continuous, *with no clear boundaries between one color and the next*, the ranges are used as only an approximation. Red is any number of similar colors evoked by light consisting predominantly of the longest wavelengths of light discernable by the human eye, in the wavelength range of approximately 630-700 nm. Longer wavelengths than this are called infrared, or *below red* and cannot be seen by human eyes. Visible wavelengths also pass through the "optical window", the region of the electromagnetic spectrum that passes largely unattenuated through the Earth's atmosphere. Clean air scatters blue light more than wavelengths toward the red, which is why the mid-day sky appears blue.

With the advent of the Boes-Stilmaker comet, this optical window was changed. The rod cells and cones in the human retina, sensitive to the wavelengths, fooled the human brain into seeing no red. Tremendous amounts of reflective carbon silicates infused into the upper atmosphere by the tail of the comet resulted in a prismatic distortion of the human visible color spectrum, and changed all human chromacity from trichromatic to dichromatic- all in one easy step.

There were, however, some exceptions...

# CHAPTER 26

## A Pigment of Your Imagination

J IMBO, BREN, JOSH, Jodie and Harold were all having dinner at the table. Harold sat next to Jimbo, who had taken a liking to Jodie's boyfriend. They were still all one big happy, ugly, family, even in a world without Red. They had fried chicken and rice for dinner and Bren's delicious Huckleberry pie for dessert. Jimbo and his Red Family always made Thursday nights Family TV Night at home. It was quality time, a time when the whole family could get together, relax, have some popcorn and cheese puffs and enjoy each other's company, through watching entertainment like movies, DVDs and TV shows. Jodie invited her boyfriend Harold over, and he became a regular. Even though the colors of things were different, they still had their Thursday night fun. That didn't change, even if there was no Red to be seen on the screen. They watched their movies and TV in shades of yellow, blue and green, just like nearly everybody on Earth. In darkness, one could almost imagine a hint of redness, but it had to be totally dark. They turned off all the lights to watch the TV show.

Tonight, they were watching an episode of *"The Adventures of Porky in the 21$^{st}$ and ¼ Century"*. The show was about the serio-comic events of Porky Parker, a fat, lonely, loveable loser. Everything that could possibly go wrong in Porky's life went wrong. This made for great TV entertainment. In this episode, Porky had just cashed a large paycheck and was heading home when he was mugged, robbed and stabbed by homeless drug addicts, then pushed off a cliff and left to die. Funny! He lay on his back mortally wounded at the bottom of the cliff, dazed and semiconscious. Night fell.

When Porky woke up, he was naked and lying on top of what looked like a Formica table. His wounds were mended and covered up with cheap bandages. Dizzy, he sat up. His wounds hurt, but he felt all right. He looked around the room. It was a mess. It smelled like a gym locker room. His vision was slightly that of a fish-eye lens. Things were distorted. The floors were linoleum. There were clothing items strewn about the room. There was a dirty sock here, a tee-shirt there, a pair of stained underwear over there. There was an old *Herman & Catnip* comic book on the floor. There were cigarette butts and marijuana roaches on the floor next to an overturned ashtray. There was an old refrigerator in the corner of the room. He went over and opened it up. Inside was a half empty bottle of *Yoo Hoo*, a carton of cottage cheese, some ketchup, dried up cheese and an unopened shrimp cocktail. Porky was hungry. He opened the cottage cheese. It was old, but edible. He grabbed the ketchup, *Yoo Hoo* and shrimp cocktail and put them on the Formica table to eat. He mixed some ketchup into the cottage cheese. He needed a bottle opener to open the shrimp cocktail. He looked around, but there was no opener anywhere. He was dimly aware of a continuing humming sound.

Porky tried to bite the lid off the shrimp cocktail and chipped a tooth. The shrimp cocktail dropped to the floor and broke, spilling the cocktail sauce and tiny shrimp. "Damn it!" he muttered. He finished the cottage cheese, washing it down with the *Yoo Hoo*. He wondered where he was. "Hello?

Anybody here?" He eyed the shrimp cocktail mess on the floor. He was still hungry, so he sat down on the floor and picked the tiny shrimp out and ate them. As he was eating the shrimps off the floor, he heard a *pssshhht!* sound. A sliding door opened, and in came two aliens. They looked like humans, except that they were green. They wore ridiculous goldfish bowl space helmets with little antennae on top. They had on ludicrous glitter vinyl uniforms with garish spray-painted gold boots. They moved and spoke in unison. They walked over to Porky, sitting on the floor. They looked at him, then at each other, and then back at him. They both switched on their translating vocoders and spoke. "What you doing?"

"Oh! Nothing!" Porky stood up, naked and embarrassed. "Why you eat our food?"

"Uh, I was so hungry, and I didn't know anybody was here. I'm sorry."

"Okay." They looked at his bandaged wounds. "You feel better now?"

"Huh? Oh. Yes, I think so— where am I?"

"You on our space ship. You like?" They smiled proudly. "We pick you up. You broke. We fix. You better now. Come sit down. We talk." The aliens led him into another room that was much cleaner than the previous room. There was laboratory equipment and other strange devices hanging on the wall, along with cheap framed prints of famous paintings. There was an elaborately framed print of poker-playing dogs. Porky was disappointed with the aliens and their spacecraft. They were nothing like the fabled aliens everybody feared and dreaded. These were just a couple of guys with a space ship that looked like a messy college dorm room. No trans-hypnotic powers. No superior technology other than the spacecraft. He noticed what looked like some kind of probing device hanging on the wall. "Nice paintings you got here!" Porky remarked sarcastically. The aliens didn't get it. "We appreciate fine art. Those real paintings, you know. We art lovers."

"Right. And what's that thing hanging there?" He pointed to the probe. The aliens looked at the probe, then at each other. "It nothing."

"Isn't that an alien probe?"

"No! It no probe, no probe at all!"

"Are you sure? It looks like an alien probe to me!"

"No probe! No probe! You sit down now." They led him to what looked like a giant half egg shell.

"Um, you got another chair? I'm afraid I might break that."

"No it Okay. Sit, sit." Porky sat down on the chair and it grew larger, accommodating his fat ass. It molded around his fat ass perfectly and surprisingly comfortably. "Oh! Thanks, that's much better." Finally some alien technology! But then, the chair grew appendages that wrapped around his arms and legs, strapping him down in the chair. "Oh, man!." He was so used to everything going wrong; he expected it at every turn. He was always right. Now he was going to get probed by aliens. The aliens came close and peered at Porky. One of them reached out and twisted his nipple. "Ow! Hey, what's the big idea?"

"So sorry." The aliens patted Porky's belly, bouncing it. They poked pinched and prodded Porky all over his body, with no comment or expression. After a few minutes they stopped and looked at each other, shaking their heads. "He too fat."

"Yeah. He too fat. He go home now." Porky grimaced. Always somebody there to tell him how fat he was. Even aliens from outer space! Everyone on earth rejected Porky; the aliens might just as well reject him, too. "We send you home now." Porky was disappointed. "You mean... that's it?"

"That is all."

"Aren't you going to probe me?"

"No probe! No probe!"

"Don't you guys probe your captives anymore?" The aliens looked at each other, and then looked away, embarrassed. "We no probe no more after we picked up small black and white stripe animal. Yeesh! No more!"

"What— you guys tried to probe a *skunk*? Bahahahahahaha!"

"Not funny. Bad smell not go away for long time. Ruin our beautiful uniforms. You smell bad, too." Porky took charge. "Well, then why the hell did you abduct me for? Look, I want answers!"

"OK, OK, we tell you. We thought you might make wubba-wubba with Cleo, but you too fat."

"Cleo?"

"Yes, Cleo— *CLEO!*" They startled Porky with their sudden shout. In a few seconds, the door slid open with a *pssshhhht!* A beautiful green-skinned woman in a sexy bikini came into the room. She wore a ridiculous goldfish bowl helmet with antennae, too. "What do you want?" she snapped, annoyed. She was in a state of languid torpor. The aliens gestured to Porky. "Wubba wubba?" The alien woman took one look at Porky. "Are you kidding? No way! Not in this galaxy!" She wheeled around and went back through the door with a *pssshhht!* Porky's fat face burned. Rejected again. *Was there no end*? "Don't feel bad. She no wubba-wubba for us, too, and we not fat, like you."

"Will you just shut the hell up about my weight? I *know* I'm overweight, Okay?"

"No, you fat... how you say...fatty fat fat...obese? Yes, you obese. We no can use you. We send you home now. Oh, first we erase your memory." They placed a tin-foil pyramid-shaped hat on Porky's head. "No! — I mean, don't erase my memory! I can make big bucks if I only had proof of alien existence!" The aliens just smiled. "You know we can no do that." They raised their memory eraser. Porky began to struggle. "No! Let me stay! I need you! I need you! Probe me! *Probe me now!*" The aliens just chuckled. "Now, now... now, now" they said and zapped his memory and sent Porky back to where they found him on the beach.

The aliens did a piss-poor job of erasing Porky's memory. Instead of remembering nothing, Porky remembered *everything*... everything except the fact that he was naked and was supposed to wear clothing. So, Porky dizzily danced naked to the pier with his tin-foil pyramid hat, politely asking men, women and children what time and day it was. He danced around the pier, amiably smiling and greeting the shocked tourists, until the police finally picked him up and took him to the station. Remembering everything, Porky blurted out his story about the robbery and stabbing, the alien abduction, the spaceship, the goldfish bowl helmets, the wubba-wubba with Cleo, the galactic space whore. He left out the part about Cleo rejecting him. He offered his tin-foil pyramid hat as proof of alien existence. The police smiled politely and nodded at Porky, but when he wasn't looking, they rolled their eyes at each other. They loved his tin-foil pyramid hat as proof of alien existence. That made their day. They could see that Porky was obviously not himself. They sent him to the hospital to properly treat his wounds. As it turned out, the police caught the homeless drug addicts and arrested them. They still had Porky's cash. After 48 hours, Porky was treated and released. They returned his money to him, gave him some clothes, and took him home. The End

Everyone laughed and had a good time, even though they couldn't see red on the screen. But they could still use their imagination and memory of what red looked like. Bren wondered aloud if the show was a little too much for Josh, who was watching on the floor, close to the screen. "What, Josh?" chuckled Jimbo. "Aw, he knows what's going on, doncha, Tiger?"

"Yeah!" said Josh, though he wasn't quite sure what he meant by that.

# CHAPTER 27

## What Was Red?

**R**ED WAS PASSION. Red was love. Red was strength. Red was depth. Red was guilt. Red was pain. Red was courage. Red was valor. Red was blood. Red was skin. Red was a Sunset. Red was a cheek. Red was anger. Red was hate. Red was hot. Red was debt. Red was Evil. Red was Papal. Red was royalty. Red was honor. Red was sacrifice. Red was hair. Red was brick. Red was the rooftop. Red was the barn. Red was a nose. Red was an eye. Red was a face. Red was raw. Red was the hand. Red was a rubber ball. Red was the Devil. Red was a cape. Red was power. Red was fire. Red was mud. Red was lipstick. Red was a fingernail. Red was Dawn. Red was a Rose. Red was a Tulip. Red was a bone. Red was a Baby Red potato. Red was an onion. Red was a tomato. Red was a cherry. Red was a raspberry. Red was an apple. Red was a pomegranate. Red was working class. Red was ketchup. Red was a cranberry. Red was a shrimp cocktail. Red was a lobster. Red was a crab. Red was a herring. Red was a back-up light. Red was Birth. Red was Death. Red was debt. Red was a dog's pecker. Red was wrath. Red was bullfighting. Red was lust. Red was the artery. Red was the heart. Red was high efficiency. Red was obtrusive.

Red was a diamond. Red was a tongue. Red was a firecracker. Red was dynamite. Red was poison. Red was a cross. Red was the Coca-Cola logo color. Red was a "STOP" sign. Red was a brake light. Red was a warning light. Red was a stop light. Red was a cardinal. Red was a Cardinal. Red was a St. Louis Cardinal. Red was a Washington Redskin. Red was a light signifying that prostitution was available within the vicinity. Red was the head of the woodpecker. Red was dye. Red was a freckle. Red was a nipple. Red was a mosquito bite. Red was a ruby. Red was a carnelian. Red was a shirt. Red was a diary. Red was a toothbrush. Red was a wagon. Red was a beret. Red was the Power Ranger. Red was a chili. Red was chili. Red was a bean. Red was cedar. Red was velvet. Red was the color of Jesus Christ's spoken words in The Bible.

Red was a car. Red was wine. Red was a pill. Red was fury. Red was rough. Red was a letter. Red was a warning. Red was shocking. Red was "warm". Red was fault. Red was excitement. Red was blame. Red was revenge. Red was sin. Red was an ember. Red was the tide. Red was the ladybug. Red was the snake. Red was the spider. Red was the scorpion. Red was the Popsicle. Red was the oven mitt. Red was a riding hood. Red was Mars. Red was a little hen. Red was dust. Red was a zone in football. Red was part of the rainbow. Red was Satan. Red was Hell. Red was war. Red was socialism. Red was glare from rockets. Red was a squirrel. Red was Kool-Aid. Red was a pack of Marlboros. Red is a tail light. Red was beauty. Red was ruddy. Red was a loss. Red was a Corvette. Red was health. Red was a deer. Red was wealth. Red was the Sun. Red was Communism. Red was soda pop. Red was cinnamon. Red was brave. Red was feisty. Red was fiery. Red was chewing gum. Red was a can of *Coke*. Red was ready for anything. Red was drawing chalk. Red was an Irish Setter. Red was American. Red was British. Red was French. Red was German. Red was the first color. Red was shame. Red was embarrassment. Red was burning. Red was medical aid. Red was a label. Red was a banner. Red was a Baron. Red was a panic button. Red was violence. Red was a nuclear missile launch button. Red was a telephone. Red was a name. Red was a telephone phone booth and double-decker bus in England. Red was Japan. Red was China. Red was a lollipop. Red was the writing pen. Red was the Bingo blotter. Red was cinnamon. Red was a fire engine. Red was a dog. Red was licorice. Red was candy. Red was Valentine's Day. Red was the Fourth of July. Red was Halloween. Red was Thanksgiving. Red was Christmas. Red was Santa Claus. Red was a ribbon. Red was Rudolph's nose. Red was a balloon. Red was a sore. Red was an EXIT sign. Red was a scratch. Red was a Robin's breast. Red was a backwards baseball cap. Red was a sock. Red was leadership. Red was heat. Red was a pin cushion. Red was a Bakelite bracelet. Red was a shoe. Red was a dress. Red was a scarf. Red was a suspender. Red was a radish. Red was a handkerchief. Red was a beet. Red was danger. Red was purity. Red was good luck. Red was happiness. Red was a Hummingbird feeder. Red was the tail of the Hawk. Red was a fox. Red was a wolf. Red was a cat. Red was a dwarf star. Red was rock. Red was a flag. Red was a laser beam. Red was infra-red. Red was a baboon's butt. Red was sunburn. Red was life. Red was a jacket. Red was scarlet. Red was pink. Red was purple. Red was rust. Red was brown. Red was flesh. Red was a key color. Red was everything. Red was *gone*.

# CHAPTER 28

## The Taking of Soleil

SOLEIL HAD JUST finished her fashion presentation at *The Whale*. She had demonstrated her new line of make-up that would cover the unsightly veins and translucency of the human body. Since there was no longer a flesh color, there were only three choices of new make-up colors available. One was a powder blue. One was pale yellow. One was light green. There was of course, white, gray and black, though black make-up on white people was considered politically incorrect. Still, some white people chose black simply because of the circumstances. It was actually quite handsome. There was black and blue lipstick for contrast There was blue eye shadow as before the absence of red….

Soleil walked out of The Whale and got into her new, formerly red Beamer. She still wore the engagement ring Martin Boes had given her on the night of the comet, even though the rubies were no longer red. She drove off, heading for the Santa Monica Freeway. Off Traction Avenue, she turned onto the long, dark, inclined freeway on-ramp. Suddenly, an SUV came up from behind her and cut in front of her, slowing down to a stop. Soleil had to brake, or crash into it. Another

SUV came up right behind her and wedged her in between the two SUV's. Sensing danger, Soleil revved the engine, trying to push the front SUV up so she could squeeze out. Her tires squealed, burning rubber. It didn't work. The SUV was too big. She threw it into reverse and tried the same thing on the rear SUV. Her tires squealed and burned tires burned She blared her horn, hoping someone would hear her and come to her aid, but there was no one there. Her car was completely wedged in. She couldn't move.

A nondescript dark suited man in a ski mask got out of the front SUV and came back towards Soleil. She auto-locked her doors and grabbed her iPhone 7. The man went to the passenger side and tried the door. Finding it locked, he made an *open up* gesture with one of his gloved hands. Soleil dialed 911 on her phone and pressed the speakerphone button. The emergency operator answered. "911,What is your emergency?"

"I'm on the Santa Monica Freeway on ramp off Traction, these men are trying to get me, I'm…" Suddenly, her ITWM windshield was smashed with a crowbar, showering Soleil with ice cubes. The man poked the crowbar through and knocked the phone out of her hand. The crowbar then smashed the hole bigger and bigger, showering her with more ice. Soleil reached under her seat and pulled up her taser weapon. She waited until the hole in the windshield was wider to get a good shot. The man kept smashing, and when he backed off for a second, she fired the taser. She got him. The taser pins stuck in his shoulder and he fell back and onto the ground, groaning and quivering. She tased him over and over. Two more nondescript men in ski masks came up and one yanked the wires of the taser, yanking the gun out of her hand while the other finished smashing her ITWM windshield. Crushed ice covered Soleil and the front seats. Soleil grabbed her knife and slashed at the four arms now trying to get her through the windshield. One arm grabbed her by her hair and pulled her up. Another arm grabbed her slashing arm and put a cloth to her face. The last thing Soleil remembered was slashing out at dark, gloved arms. The four arms pulled Soleil out through the windshield, put her into the back of the front SUV and took off. The tased Nondescript man was writhing and twitching beside Soleil's Beamer. Another nondescript man walked over to him and drew a gun. *"No! No! Don't! Don't shoot!"* cried the twitching man. The gunman fired one shot into the head of the twitching man, killing him. He was expendable. Then the gunman got into his SUV. He pulled out, tires screeching, and they were gone.

# CHAPTER 29

## Ain't Been Nothin' But the Blues
## Since They Took Away My Red

SOME SAID IT was God's punishment. Some said it was Allah's punishment. Some said it was Yahweh's punishment. Some said it was Shiva's punishment. Some said it was the Great Spirit's punishment. Some said it was joke by Buddha. Some say it was the Harvest God's punishment. Some said it was the Apocalypse. Some say it was Armageddon. Some said it was Doomsday. Some said it would lead to the extinction of the human race, like the dinosaurs. Some said it was punishment for gay acceptance. Some said it was punishment for gay intolerance. Some said it was God's punishment for building a mosque near Ground Zero at the Twin Towers site.

But what was done, was done. Red had been taken away from the world, and there was no telling how long it would take for Red to come back, *if* it came back. Meanwhile, the world would have to get back to business as usual. Just because people were color-blind, didn't mean they could just quit. Just because everyone appeared as pasty ogres didn't mean they could just pack it in. Just because the skies were green and the trees were blue, that didn't make someone special. People would have to deal with it, live with it, go through it, and cope with it. They had no choice. And so they did.

It was thought at the beginning that all human eyes had lost the ability to see red and the other colors correctly, but as time went on, it would be discovered that a very small percentage of people on earth could perceive red, but the figures were not yet determined.

Everyone's faces appeared to be covered with unsightly veins, so soon there were new facial and body make-up powders to cover up the veins. People had some new, exciting choices in make-up. They had their choices of powder blue, yellow, dark blue, dark green, pale green, white and black. Yellow was the most popular color other than blue. The new make-ups became fashion statements, but then, class distinctions would develop, like the *blues* versus the *yellows*, for example. Then there were those who believed in their own natural gray skin color, veins and all.

Fashion would suffer greatly without Red. The late night talk show hosts started making jokes in their monologues about the loss of Red. After all, they were affected, too. There were endless joke possibilities about the absence of red, and much great material was gleaned from the taking of Red. This did make people feel better, but the truth was, it was no laughing matter. The absence of Red would prove to be not funny… not funny at all. The laughter would stop, soon. Some very unfunny things would happen from not being able to see Red. There would be trouble ahead in a World Without Red. The world was getting… *colder*. But things had to go on. Ron survived his suicide attempt only to take the challenge of living in a World Without Red. The Garden Gnome never lost a beat in mowing his lawn every day, still tackling it like a terrier, making his new blue lawn the best blue lawn in the county. He drove around in his formerly Candy Apple Red '64 Sting Ray, which was now *pale gray*. But it still worked fine. He repainted it Metallic Blue. The President of the United States was under fire for not telling the public about how close the Boes-Stilmaker comet would come to Earth. Impeachment proceedings were considered.

---

The King of the Blues, the legendary Blues Singer/Guitarist with the guitar named "Lucille" was despondent over the loss of the color Red after all these years. This time, he *really* had the blues! In order to climb out of his funk, he wrote and sang a brand new Blues song and video, with an All-Star line-up of other Blues giants with special guest stars. The video was seventeen minutes long, and each star had their own solo turns. They all shared the Blues of *No Red*. His plaintive guitar and soaring vocals spoke out to the world about the unjust color changes and the tragic loss of Red. The word, "they" was just a song writing device, of course- it was an "it" that took away his Red. But it made people feel better if they could blame the taking of Red on "them" instead of a cosmic event. That's what The Blues was for!

The *"Ain't Been Nothin' But the Blues Since They Took Away My Red"* video and song was a tremendous hit worldwide, his all-time biggest seller and the crowning achievement of his long, illustrious career. It was an award-winning favorite in all the bars, lounges and honky-tonks. Millions of copies sold worldwide. He donated the profits to all worldwide charities, including the *Red Cross*, which by the way, was now the *White Cross* temporarily, until Red decided to come back. But they still referred to it as the *Red Cross*. Other musicians followed with their own Red ballads and laments. An All-Star benefit concert was announced, with the proceeds donated to all worldwide charities to aid in adjusting to the new color rules, and for research in bringing back the correct human visual color spectrum. How this would be accomplished was unknown, at this time. It was going to take a lot more than a song to bring back Red.

# CHAPTER 30

## World Without Red

Red Was *Gone!* Gone from sight. That is, all things that were previously known to be red colored, now appeared to be gray. Red was gone from human vision. Not only red, but the tints and hues and pigments of red were gone, too. Gone! were *Red, Pink, Orange, Brown, Purple, Violet, Burgundy, Cerise, Dusty Rose, Maroon, Crimson, Scarlet, Brick, Oxblood, Carmine, Vermilion, Ochre, Iron Oxide (Rust), Puce, Alizarin, Magenta, Fuchsia and Candy Apple Red.*

Horrifyingly, human skin that was once flesh colored now appeared gray, with blue-green veins and arteries most apparent all over the body. The loss of red tint gave the human skin a most unattractive translucency, with inner organs discernable upon close inspection. The effect was shocking and appalling to everyone. Everyone on the surface of the Earth was gray with blue veins. Light and pale skinned people got the worst of it. Dark-skinned persons fared better, their veins were not so apparent. No one escaped this affliction, not being able to see Red.

*Everyone*— man, woman, and child, was robbed of the ability to see Red. *Everyone*. The Butcher, the Baker, the

Candlestick Maker. Rich man, Poor man, Beggar man, Thief, Doctor, Lawyer, Indian Chief. Every Tom, Dick and Harry. Every Sally, Sue and Mary.

*Everywhere*—in New York, London, Paris, Munich, Caracas, La Paz, Washington D.C., Buenos Aires, Newfoundland, Oslo, Hong Kong, Las Vegas, Kamloops, Brasilia, Azores, Lisbon, Berlin, Warsaw, Budapest, Prague, Rome, Athens, Helsinki, Istanbul, Capetown, Moscow, Jeddah, Tehran, Abu Dhabi, Kabul, Islamabad, Tashkent, Ekaterinburg, Mumbai, Colombo, Kathmandu, Dhaka, Novosibirsk, Bangkok, Hanoi, Krasnoyarsk, Beijing, Tokyo, Seoul, Adelaide, Guam, Sydney, Jakarta, Canberra, Auckland, Samoa, Midway, Honolulu, Los Angeles, Denver, Phoenix, Chicago, Detroit, Dallas, Irkutsk, Vancouver, Rabat, Philadelphia, Tel Aviv, Helena, Moose Jaw, Tokyo, Honolulu, the Virgin Islands, Bakersfield, Glasgow, Christchurch, New Delhi, Seattle, and Manchester. All over the world. The people in these cities *could not see red.*

All automobiles that were painted Red, now appeared to be painted gray. Stop lights and "STOP" signs were now changed to blue. Formerly Red Brick buildings were now gray. Bren's Red-breasted Robins were now Bren's Gray-breasted Robins. Coke cans were changed to blue. Campbell's soup cans were changed to blue. Jodie's sexy red leather diary was now gray leather. Josh's red plastic toothbrush was now gray plastic. Red wine was clear. Red wagons were changed to blue. Red-hot chili peppers were now gray Red-hot chili peppers. Red sunsets were now green sunsets. Red ketchup was changed to green.. But this was not all that had changed in the human visual color spectrum.

*Everything that once was blue was now green. And everything that once was green was now blue.* The skies now appeared green. The grass, trees and vegetation now appeared blue. The oceans ranged from green to teal. If there really was Blue grass in Kentucky, it was now green, but it could still keep its state motto, "The Bluegrass State", because all the grass in Kentucky and everywhere else was now truly blue. But the absence of Red was the killer. *Bad enough that the sky is green and the grass is blue. OK, OK, OK, we can live with that. But Red! Red! Where the hell is Red?* Red was *gone!* Actually, it was still there. it just couldn't be seen.

People who were underground when the color change occurred could still see red; but if they emerged to the surface into sunlight, their brains would adjust to the new color rules, and they would also lose their capability to see red. All the scientists and color theorists were helpless when it came to the absence of red. There was nothing they could do about it. Green and blue could be adjusted, as far as that went. But the color red could not be recreated. For one thing, *red could not be seen*. How could you mix red when you could not see it? Red could not be visibly recreated, because there was no reference to red. *No one could see red, now.* Not on TV, not on saved files on the best computers. When one went to choose the color red from the color palette on their computer, all they could see were gray swatches where red swatches used to be. It was a disastrous day for movies and TV. All the movies on DVDs, Blue-ray, VHS and in theaters were all without Red. They were ruined. They all might as well have been filmed in black and white, which incidentally, many people adapted to their affliction by viewing their DVDs in black and white. At least there was some nostalgic cinematic element of *film noir* pleasure in B&W, rather than films in the awful grays yellows, greens and blues. Just as in real life, the movies showed people as ghastly gray ghouls with veins. People with red hair now appeared to have dark hair. Internet pornography suffered. Who wanted to look at nude pictures of big-breasted, gray skinned, splotchy, veiny models? Red was *gone!* Scarlet was gone. Gone with the wind. Gone, like Soleil. So was beauty on earth. It was very dull and drab without red. After eons, the sky was now green, the trees were now blue, and there was no red. Red was *gone!*

The World was beginning to recover from the initial shock of the new color rules. People were beginning to cope and adjust to a world without Red. They had to. There was no choice in the matter. Many people imagined that they could see red, but it was only their imagination.

The President's heart-felt speech at least gave hope to carry on. There was the raised expectation that the colors would eventually return to normal with the dissipation of the reflective dust layer trapped in the upper atmosphere to the edge of space. But the Powers That Be were never clear when that might happen. They didn't know. Professor Stilmaker didn't know. Martin Boes didn't know. It might take weeks. It might take months. It might take years. It might take decades. It might take centuries. It might take a millennium. It might never happen. They didn't know. The loss of Red and the other color changes would soon prove to be more than just an inconvenience. It would turn life into an utter living nightmare, both physically and mentally, for nearly everyone on Earth, although nobody knew it yet. Suffice to say, that the color Red was now indeed, a pigment of your imagination.

END OF BOOK ONE

# AFTERWORD

---

*I long for days when skies were blue,*
*For dawn and sunset's golden hue*
*When trees were brown and grass was green*
*And Red was there, and ever seen*

*But now I sing a different tune,*
*Of no more golden afternoons*
*For green is blue and blue is green,*
*And Red is there, but never seen*